JFK to Dublin

By:

Brooke St. James

No part of this book may be used or reproduced in any form or by any means without prior written permission of the author.

Copyright © 2016

Brooke St. James

All rights reserved.

Other titles available from Brooke St. James:

Another Shot:
A Modern-Day Ruth and Boaz Story

When Lightning Strikes

Something of a Storm (All in Good Time #1)
Someone Someday (All in Good Time #2)

Finally My Forever (Meant for Me #1)
Finally My Heart's Desire (Meant for Me #2)
Finally My Happy Ending (Meant for Me #3)

Shot by Cupid's Arrow

Dreams of Us

Meet Me in Myrtle Beach (Hunt Family #1)
Kiss Me in Carolina (Hunt Family #2)
California's Calling (Hunt Family #3)
Back to the Beach (Hunt Family #4)
It's About Time (Hunt Family #5)

Loved Bayou (Martin Family #1)
Dear California (Martin Family #2)
My One Regret (Martin Family #3)
Broken and Beautiful (Martin Family #4)
Back to the Bayou (Martin Family #5)

Almost Christmas

Chapter 1

I assumed I wasn't supposed to hear the guy behind me when he whispered obscenities to his friend regarding what he wanted to do to me and some other girl who was standing next to me. Or maybe I was supposed to hear—either way I ignored them. I just stared straight ahead, inching closer to the curb as I waited for the light to change.

They were being completely inappropriate. My heart raced and blood rose to my cheeks as I felt myself becoming angrier and angrier by the second. It was that feeling you get when you're just about to have a confrontation, and I had to take a second to remind myself that there didn't have to be a confrontation if I simply continued to ignore them.

It was difficult, though. So many things had been building up prior to this moment that I felt like I could snap and turn around, swinging my bag while screaming at them. In a nutshell, the current situation with the knuckleheads behind me was basically the nail in the coffin on my opinion of men in general.

Let's pause for a brief moment to reflect upon what had me so jaded.

Number 1:

My father, Saul Spicer. The same Emmy-winning Saul Spicer who has produced mega-hit television dramas for the last two decades—the one who recently got charged with sexual harassment by one of the actresses on his show. He was acquitted, and in the long run, nothing will change for him professionally, but it was all over the news, and as my mom says, "our family name will forever be tainted by this". She publically forgave him, and as far as the media was concerned, we were one big happy reformed family, which was somewhat true since we never had what you would call a normal family life to begin with. I heard my brother saying he thought my parents were just staying married for financial reasons, but they never really discussed it with us. We knew about as much as the media did.

So, was it cool to grow up with a successful TV producer for a dad? Yes. Was he a faithful husband to my mother? No.

Moving on to the Number 2 reason I'm jaded about men:

Brian Rosenberg.

I dated him for a year in high school only to find out that he was sleeping with other girls behind my back. He said it was, "what I got for making him wait so long," and the funny thing was that I didn't even realize he was in such a hurry.

Number 3:

Cameron Harrison.

This one was different.

This one stung.

I thought he was the one.

Cameron and I dated my whole junior and senior year of college, and had even begun making plans to get married. We were together when all that stuff with my dad went down, and I really thought we were in it for the long haul. That was before I caught him in his apartment with another girl and not much clothing.

There was a huge scene where he first attempted to say it wasn't what it looked like, but since that was ludicrous, he changed his approach, to trying to make it seem like the whole thing was my fault. He said he wanted to marry a girl like me, but that the idea of not having sex before we got married was ridiculous and old fashioned. He added that I was cruel for not recognizing and meeting a man's basic needs. It was terrible. I was so traumatized by him that I now had a strict no-dating policy.

So, you see, those guys on the street corner were simply messing with the wrong girl. I was sick and tired of men and their one-track minds. I clinched my fists, praying those morons behind me wouldn't say anything else before I could walk away.

I got my wish. The light changed, and before I knew it, the whole mass of people on the corner stepped out to cross the street, and I got lost in the front of the pack, leaving the offending guys behind. I used my best speed-walking skills to get as far from them as possible, continuing two more blocks before making it to the Mexican restaurant where I was meeting some friends for lunch.

Lu was the only one there when I arrived. She was inside, but I could see her through the windows as I walked in front of the restaurant. She waved at me, and I smiled and waved back, although it wasn't very convincing because I was trying to pay attention to where I was walking, and I was still annoyed at the guys from the crosswalk. I told the hostess that I already knew where I was going, and she gestured for me to go right ahead.

"Macy is on her way," Lu said as she motioned for me to sit next to her. "And Drake's here. He went to use the restroom. I think his new girlfriend's coming." She smiled as I took a seat at the round table. There was a basket of chips in the center, and I took one of them, scooping up some salsa before popping it into my mouth.

"What's up?" she asked, knowing my smile was slightly forced.

I rolled my eyes and shrugged. "A couple of guys were mouthing off on the street. They were standing behind me, explicitly referring to body parts as power tools."

"How charming," Lu said, laughing a little before she crunched down on a chip. She gestured over my shoulder. "There's Drake."

I turned just in time to see our friend, Drake, walking up behind me. I stood and hugged him before he sat at the table with us.

"Whazzuup?" he asked, smiling and bobbing his head in a silly way at me once he sat down. "I'm so glad we came here. I love this place." He pinched my arm. "What have you been up to, Ms. Sarah-cakes?"

"Sarah was just telling me about a couple of real winners she ran into at Home Depot on her way here," Lu said. "I think she got their number."

I laughed and shook my head, but I was chewing a bite of food, so I didn't say anything.

"They weren't at Home Depot, but they were trying to score with her by referring to their body parts as tools," she explained, causing Drake to make a distasteful face.

"Me or the girl standing next to me," I said.

Lu gave me a smirk before looking at Drake. "She thinks it's all men who are scumbags, but I tell her she just sees the worst of them because of how hot she is."

I giggled and rolled my eyes at Lu, who was grinning at me.

"Her therapist even came on to her," she added. "Men just can't help themselves."

"Oh my gosh, I forgot about that." I said.

"Your *therapist* hit on you?" Drake asked, staring at me with a curious smile as he held a chip in mid-air. "Isn't that illegal?"

"He talked in code," Lu explained with such confidence it was as if she had been there, which she hadn't.

Drake looked at me, and I nodded. "He said he had an idea for a storyline for one of Dad's shows," I said. "He explained details of an affair two of the characters would have."

"What'd you say?" Drake asked, with a huge, amused grin.

I shrugged. "I was so taken aback by him suggesting a risqué storyline, that I didn't even realize he was talking to me in code. I just smiled and agreed to everything he was saying, thinking he was seriously trying to talk to me about Dad's work."

"Why were you even seeing a therapist?" Drake asked.

"My mom set it up after everything happened with my dad."

"Are you going back there?" he asked.

"No."

He shrugged. "It must be terrible not being able to go three feet without guys hitting on you."

"That's what I'm saying," Lu added. "She's too hot. She needs to tone it down a little bit. Maybe put on a turtle neck or mess up your hair a little."

I gave them a huge smile, knowing I had a chunk of salsa spread across my front teeth—I could feel it. "That helps," Drake said, shielding his eyes like he could hardly stand to look at me.

"Tell her there are good guys out there," Lu said, talking to Drake.

Drake looked at me. "I'm a good guy," he said.

"Drake's a good guy," Lu confirmed.

"I know he is, and even still, I've witnessed a few broken hearts in his wake."

"Aww, come on," Drake defended, smiling. Then he grew serious and mumbled, "Okay, no more broken heart talk," as a cute blonde made her way to the table wearing a bright smile. I thought she must be the next in line.

Thankfully, I remembered the salsa in my teeth, and was able to clear it away before she made it to the table. Her name was Beckett, and Lu and I both smiled and agreed it was a pleasure to meet her when Drake made introductions.

We had a fine time getting to know Drake's new lady. She was quirky and beautiful just like the six or eight who had come before her. Macy showed up right after Beckett, and since Macy sort of stole the show everywhere she went, Beckett settled blissfully into the background near Drake's side.

Lu, Drake, Macy, and I all went to the School of Arts at Columbia and had been close friends the whole time we were there. Lu moved in with me after we graduated, so she and I still saw each other all the time, but it had been a while since I had seen Macy or Drake, and it was great to catch up with them.

Macy wore her hair in a huge mass of curls that appeared to stand on end in a circular shape around her head, and she had a big, vibrant personality to go with her appearance. Everyone loved Macy. She was known for telling it like it was in the most hilarious ways, and I missed seeing her more regularly like I did in college.

"Did you tell them the good news yet?" Macy asked, looking at Lu who stared back at her with a confused expression.

We were about halfway through our meal at that point, and the question had come out of nowhere.

"What good news?" Lu asked.

"About S&S."

"What about it?" Lu asked with wide eyes.

"You got an interview," Macy said.

Lu's face lit up.

"I texted you about it this morning."

"I didn't get it," Lu said, digging in her purse for her phone.

"Is it a job interview?" Beckett asked, having no idea what S&S was.

"Shower & Shelter," Macy explained.

Beckett smiled and nodded as if she recognized the name. "Art gallery, right? I think I've seen that."

"There's a gallery," Macy said, "but that's only half of it."

Beckett raised her eyebrows in a way that said she was intrigued.

"That's why it's called Shower & Shelter." Macy said. "Do you know anything about it?"

Beckett shook her head.

"I live there. It's basically free housing for artists. The owner of it is an artist, but also an art collector and seller—that's how he made his millions. His name is Theo Duval. He speaks French and English. He grew up in Montreal, but he came to

New York when he was sixteen. His parents died in a car accident, and he took a bus to New York with the cash payout of what they left him, which was four thousand dollars after their debts were paid. He felt inspired by the city and driven to create art, but it was impossible for him to devote time to creating when he had to work a full-time job and could barely make ends meet. He often thought that if only he had access to a shower and a shelter, he could devote himself to honing his skills as an artist. It was something he desired so fervently that he set a goal to be the one to provide exactly that to other people in his position."

Macy paused and put her straw to her lips, taking a sip of her soda, but we were all eating, and all of us wanted her to continue.

"He started making a little money on his art, which he turned into more money by learning how to buy and sell other people's art. He's one of those industrious workaholic types. He's probably a billionaire by now. Anyway, last year, he made good on that promise he made years before. He bought a whole building in the Upper East Side, and now, he houses thirty artists."

"You mean the one with the gallery?" Beckett asked.

Macy nodded. "So, here's what he did... he left floors 3 through 16 alone," she said, gesturing with her hand to a block of space in front of her. "They were apartments, and he just left them like they were when he bought the building. He gutted the first and second stories, though."

"For the gallery?" Beckett assumed.

"The gallery's on the first. The second floor is artist housing. There used to be twenty apartments on that floor, and he had it gutted and completely redesigned. The entire second floor is set up to house thirty artists at any given time, and everybody loves it there, so it's almost impossible to get an opening. We all have our own individual loft, and there's a huge, shared studio space. It's called the Shower & Shelter Artist Collective. It was what Mr. Duval set out to do. The gallery part of it was actually an afterthought."

"And they have an opening for Lu?" I asked Macy.

She smiled and nodded.

"To live there?" Beckett asked.

Macy nodded again. "I was wondering why she hadn't told you guys."

"I didn't see the text," Lu said, staring down at her phone.

"I saw Lane this morning," Macy said. "He said they had an opening coming up, and they were planning on calling you with the group of people they're interviewing."

Chapter 2

"I'm nervous," Lu said, stashing her phone in her purse.

Macy shook her head. "Don't be. They're gonna love you. If you don't get the spot, it's just because someone else who was closer to Mr. Duval had someone applying."

Lu took a deep breath as if everything hinged on this interview.

"You know you can stay with me as long as you need to," I said.

Lu's parents had scraped by to pay for her room and board at school, but she had been staying mostly with me since we graduated. Rent in the city was expensive, and Lu wasn't selling much of her art, not yet, at least. She often talked about moving back to New Jersey with her parents, but I knew she would hate to do that.

"I know you're not trying to kick me out or anything, but wouldn't it be cool if I got into S&S? I'd have my own space, and you'd have yours. Can you believe I got an interview?"

"I want you to have your own space and everything, I just don't understand about the free rent thing. I don't want you owing that guy anything."

Everyone sitting around the table looked at me watching confused expressions.

"I'm just saying…" I defended with my hands up. "What's in it for him?"

"He's a philanthropist," Macy said as if that was obvious.

"That's exactly what I'm afraid of," I said, pretending to mistake the word philanthropist for philanderer.

Macy, who may or may not have gotten my joke, narrowed her eyes at me in a teasing way before she added, "His goal is to help artists because he wished someone would have done the same for him."

I shrugged, feeling not so convinced. "Lu said there's a communal kitchen and bathroom," I said, showing my skepticism with my expression. I didn't mean to rain on their parade, but really, from what I knew of men, I was afraid of Lu being in a communal shower situation.

"Have you seen upstairs?" Macy asked.

I shook my head.

"It's not Sodom and Gomorrah in there. It's nice. The men's and women's areas are on opposite ends, and there's always someone working." Macy paused and cocked her head at me as if trying to remember something. "Are you sure you haven't seen it?"

I shook my head. "I've been to the gallery, but never upstairs."

"Well, you wouldn't be worried about it if you had ever been up there. It's legit."

I smiled and nodded, but I still wasn't quite convinced, and my friends could see it.

"She thinks guys only have one thing on their mind." Lu explained. "No offense, Drake."

Just then, a man walked up to our table. I turned to stare at him, noticing right away that he was sharply dressed and wearing a confident grin.

"Can I take that for you?" he asked, reaching out for Drake's empty plate. I was full, so I went ahead and handed him my plate as well. We made eye contact as he took it from me, and I marveled at how polished a table-busser he was.

"What are you thinking when you look at Sarah here?" Macy asked, obviously talking to the guy.

I glanced at her with a terrified expression, even though I had no idea where she was headed with the question. She had asked it loudly enough that we all turned to look at her, and she stared straight at the ruggedly handsome bus boy who was now holding our used dishes. He smiled curiously at her, and she reached out to pat my back, causing him to glance at me.

"This is Sarah," she said, horrifying me. "Would you mind telling us what you were thinking just now when you were staring at her?"

"Macy!" I whispered.

She smiled at me and gestured toward the guy. "I just wanted to know what he had on his mind when you two were looking at each other." She turned to face him. "I was trying to see if she was right about guys, that's all."

"Oh, my goodness, you need to leave that poor man alone, Macy." I shook my head as I lowered my gaze, putting my fingertips and thumb on my eyebrows and waiting for him to walk away.

He did not do as I hoped. Instead, he stood there. "I don't mind telling you what I was thinking, but if something's awkward..." He trailed off, and I knew he was looking at me. I could feel it.

"Nothing's awkward," Macy assured him. She nudged me with her elbow, and I glanced up to smile at the guy, feeling red-faced and horrified.

He wore a curious half-smile as he stared at me, letting his light eyes roam all over my face. I blinked and stared down shyly. "I was thinking she looked like sunshine, actually."

That caused me to cut my eyes at him, which made his smile broaden as he shrugged.

"It's true. You look like sunshine to me. It was the very first thing that crossed my mind when I was standing here just now. I was trying to think of something better to say, but you really do strike me as sunshine."

"In a fat way?" I asked, wrinkling my nose at him and hoping my off-the-wall comment would serve as distraction to my pounding heart.

"No," he said with an amused grin. "In a sunny way."

"I can totally see what you're saying!" Lu said.

"Me too," Macy added.

I looked at all of them as if they had gone mad. "You all think I'm fat," I said with a fake pouty face. My weight had fluctuated a little over the years, but I had never been self conscious about it. I was totally kidding, and they all knew it.

"Were you thinking about hooking up with her?" Macy asked.

"Macy!" I scolded again, with wide eyes.

"I'm pretty sure that's a trick question," the guy said.

I glanced at him with an apologetic stare. "Yes, please don't answer that. They're just giving me a hard time today." He smiled at me and let our eyes stay connected for several seconds before shifting to arrange the empty dishes in his hands. Within seconds, they were balanced, and he glanced at everyone at the table. "How was your meal?"

"Amazing," Drake said.

"Seriously," Lu added. "It's my new favorite."

"I'm glad to hear that," he said with another smile.

His teeth weren't perfectly straight, but they were even more appealing just the way they were. There was a little bit of sharpness to his canines that gave his smile a dangerous edge. I swallowed hard and glanced away when I caught myself staring at his mouth.

"Can I take anyone else's plate?" he asked.

Beckett handed hers over, and he took it.

"I'll eat that," Drake said, reaching out to intercept the plate, which still had about half of her portion remaining.

"I was going to ask if you wanted me to box it," the busser said.

"I'll eat it," Drake said, looking at Beckett, who smiled and nodded as if she was fine with him finishing it off.

"I'm glad you kept it," Beckett said, reaching over to take another bite of food off of the plate that was now in front of Drake. "I just got so caught up in him being Collin Ross that I handed him my plate. I think I just wanted to say I handed him something."

"You talking about..." Drake motioned with a thumb in the direction the guy had walked away.

"I *thought* I recognized him," Lu said.

Drake looked over his shoulder. "Is he famous or something?"

"He owns like ten restaurants," Beckett said. She looked around. "This must be one of them. I don't think he's a chef, but he's a famous food guy for sure. He's always a guest judge on all those Food Network shows."

"I've seen him!" Macy said.

"I have too," Lu said. "And he's even hotter in person."

"He's not that hot," Beckett said rolling her eyes for Drake's sake.

"I can't believe you put him on the spot like that," I said, kicking Macy under the table.

"Oh, but it would have been okay if he was a waiter?" Macy teased, dodging me.

"No, but better than some Food Network guy."

"You thought he was cute," Lu said, teasing me. "You liked that he called you sunshine."

"No I didn't," I said defensively.

"You did!" Lu teased.

Macy put the back of her hand to her forehead and swooned dramatically. "I don't know what I would give to be called a beautiful ray of sunshine," she said in her best Scarlett O'Hara voice. She winked at me. "Don't try to act like you didn't see how he was looking at you—how you were looking at each other."

"We were looking at each other like we were mortified by *you* putting him on the spot like that."

"She didn't put him on the spot until after you were staring," Drake interjected, being no help whatsoever.

"I can't believe you had a moment with *Collin Ross*," Beckett said longingly, causing Drake to scowl at her, which made us all laugh.

My heart was beating a mile a minute as I tried to remember the details of the conversation, but everyone was still talking, and I wasn't able to rehash everything.

"Are you guys ready for the check, or would you like to order some dessert?" our server asked, coming to stand over Drake's shoulder so we could all see her. "And Mr. Ross said your appetizers are on the house."

"Tell him he can have Sarah's number if he wants," Macy said, which resulted in my elbow coming into contact with her arm.

Our server just laughed nervously as she leaned over to take Lu's plate. "Are you Sarah Spicer?" she asked, glancing at me with a shy smile.

I nodded.

"I usually don't do things like this, but I'm really hoping I get a part on your dad's new pilot. I auditioned a few days ago, and I think I really nailed the part. Do you think you could put in a good word for me?"

And there it was. The phrase I had heard countless other times. Everybody wanted me to *put in a good word* with my dad. I just smiled and nodded since that was easier than explaining that my dad had nothing to do with casting.

"I'm Nichole Massey. I read for the part of Elle. I had my hair in a big bun."

I smiled and nodded.

"Thank you so much!" she said.

"I can't promise anything."

"I know. I guess I just figured it couldn't hurt to ask."

"Certainly can't hurt," I said, feeling bad that she was so excited and nervous to talk to me about it.

"I figured I might as well since I'm on a roll today," she said, leaning over to pick up the remaining dishes. "Mr. Ross is here today, and I overheard him talking about filming an episode of Best Chef tonight. I asked if he'd take me on the set, and he agreed." She shrugged. "I'm trying to break through into show business any way I can. If I don't try to make the most of any given situation, well then that's on me."

"You go girl," Macy said, snapping her fingers in mid-air the way they did in the 90's.

They all seemed to like the gutsy waitress, and I liked her, too. Only for some reason I had an odd sense of jealousy that she was going somewhere with the handsome restaurant owner when I wasn't—like she was somehow on my turf. My first thought was that I would show her who's boss by not putting a good word in with my dad, but then I realized that it was a ridiculous thought since her good fortune of going on the set of Best Chef was of no consequence to me. I laughed at myself internally for being jealous over this guy's attention now that I knew he was some hotshot Food Network guy. I thought about the ridiculousness of me wanting his attention at all. My own feelings left me a little confused, and I sat there, composing myself.

Chapter 3

Drake and Beckett had to leave, but Macy and Lu decided to stay for coffee and dessert, so I stayed with them.

"Ooh, they missed the best part," Macy said, taking a huge bite of the soft sopaipilla with a blissful expression.

"I thought she was nice," Lu said, referring to Beckett.

I nodded. "Me too. I think he likes her, too."

Macy dipped a second sopaipilla in honey and stared longingly at it, like she hadn't eaten a day in her life.

"I can't believe you're still hungry," I said, since I was stuffed from lunch.

"It's the cinnamon," she said. "I have a thing for cinnamon."

I reached out to touch the top of the small French press that was sitting in front of me. "Will you push this down in like two minutes?" I asked. "I need to go use the restroom."

Lu nodded and waved me off as she chewed.

I saw Collin Ross standing in the dining room as I made my way through the restaurant in search of the ladies room. He was talking to three people who were sitting at a table, but he glanced in my direction when my movement caught his eye. He smiled and lifted his chin at me before focusing again on the people who were talking to him.

I was only in the restroom for a minute, so I was a bit surprised to see Collin standing in a completely different spot when I was on the way back to my table. He was again speaking with people at a table, but this time, he was much closer to the main walking path that led through the center of the dining room. I would have to pass right by him to get to my table, and this idea left me feeling unnerved. I told myself to breathe and put one foot in front of the other.

I thought I might make it past Collin without incident, but I was mistaken. He asked the customers sitting around the table to excuse him, and he stepped in front of me just before I made it past them.

"Hey," he said. "I'm sorry if it was weird back there. I wanted to say the right thing for you in front of your friends, but all I could see was the sun."

I put a hand to my chest, feeling altogether breathless after having him stand there, smiling and talking to me like that. "What? Me? You mean what you said at the table?" I cleared my throat in an effort to stop stuttering. "I'm the one who should be sorry about that."

Collin put a hand on my arm to usher me to the side. "I'm sorry I called you sunshine," he said. "I realized after I walked off that you may get offended by that. I was just looking at your sweater, and the way your hair's pulled up, and your smile. You just reminded me of sunshine, that's all."

"I wasn't offended by it. I figured it made sense for you to compliment your customers."

"I don't subscribe to flattery," he said with a subtle shake of his head. "I've actually never told anyone they look like sunshine—although no one has ever really asked me what I was thinking when I first laid eyes on someone."

"Sorry about that," I said.

"Let me buy you dinner to make it up to you," he said.

I smiled. "But I'm the one apologizing."

"Then you can buy me dinner," he said, carefully inspecting every inch of my face in spite of the busy restaurant.

"I'm not sure if you're asking me on a date right now, but if so, the answer is 'no' because I don't date." I could have been really tempted to go out with him, but I was so scared of falling in love and getting hurt, that I made the statement without even thinking about it.

"Why not? Are you married?"

"No. I just don't want to. I have trust issues. I'm afraid it'd be a waste of your time." I pulled back, staring at him skeptically. "Why are you asking? Do you know my dad or something?"

He threw his hands up like he had no idea what I was talking about and smiled. "Can't a guy ask a girl on a date in his own restaurant?"

I giggled. "I don't date, but thank you. I'm honored, since I heard you're some big shot up-and-comer."

"Who you callin' an up-and-comer?" he asked, staring sideways at me, and causing me to laugh again.

I smiled as I turned to walk away, I really regretted mentioning my dad, and I was glad he hadn't asked me about it. I was so used to people being nice to me because of who my dad was that, by instinct, I had to go ahead and call him out on it.

"Who's your dad?" he asked, reading my mind before I could walk away. He reached out to usher me to the side again as someone passed.

"You tell me," I said, turning to face him.

"Chuck Norris?" he asked as if it were truly his best guess.

I giggled. "Never mind," I said shaking my head shyly.

"Tell me," he said.

"No."

"Why?"

"Because he's not nearly as cool as Chuck Norris."

"Charles Schwab?" he guessed.

I smiled. "Maybe a little cooler than Charles Schwab."

He motioned with his hands for me to tell him. "Saul Spicer," I said.

"The *Bad Medicine* guy?" he asked, referring to my dad's most famous television series that was currently in its twelfth season.

I nodded.

"I think I've actually met your dad a time or two at charity functions," he said.

"Probably," I agreed. "My mom's always got us going to one of those things. In fact, I'm sure we've met before." I gestured back and forth from me to him, and he shook his head.

"I'd remember," he said, staring at me in a way that made me know he was intrigued by the looks of my face. "What's your name?"

"Sarah."

"Sarah," he repeated. "I'm Collin."

I nodded since I already knew.

"One coffee, Sarah Spicer," he said.

I shook my head regretfully. "I really don't date," I said. "I'm flattered that you'd even ask. I know my refusal only makes me seem more appealing, and I'm sorry about that. I apologize if I gave you the wrong idea. I really don't date. It's sort of a rule."

"A rule from your dad?" he asked.

"No," I said, laughing. We had drifted to the side where we were no longer in anyone's way. "I'm a grown woman. My dad didn't even care who I was dating even when I lived at home, much less now that I have my own place."

I had been living in my own apartment for the last five years, and there I was, sounding like a teenager who had just gotten my own place yesterday. I smiled and reminded myself there was no shame in being quiet, so I clamped my mouth shut and smiled at him.

"Am I to understand, Miss Spicer, that you can't have coffee with me because of a *self-inflicted* rule against dating?"

I smiled. "Yes."

He rubbed his jaw, which was lined with a week's worth of stubble—a short beard.

"I'm happy to tell you that the beauty of self-imposed rules is that you can break them," he said.

I smiled because I just couldn't help it. He was so charming that I almost forgot all about my no-dating policy.

"I won't break it," I said, knowing it was the truth. After my dad, and then Brian and Cameron, I had no desire to mess with men. I shook my head with a regretful smile.

"Why not?" he asked.

"Because you're too ugly," I said. I delivered the statement with a straight face, but I knew he knew I was joking by the way he struggled not to smile.

"That's why I need you," he said. "I need some beauty to balance out what an ugly oaf I am."

"So ugly," I said, with obvious sarcasm since he had a face that was clearly made for television. "Nichole will help," I said. "She's pretty enough."

"Who's Nichole?" he asked.

"The girl who's going with you to the set of Best Chef tonight."

"Oh, yeah. She's not coming *with* me. I'm leaving her a pass at the door."

"She's pretty, though," I said. "What I'm saying is that she could balance you out if you're looking for someone to do that."

"I'm not really looking for someone," he said.

I narrowed my eyes at him, which made him smile.

"Please say I am the first in line when you come to your senses and start breaking this despicable rule."

"I'm not breaking it."

"But I'm first in line if you do."

I smiled. "Sure. I better let you get back," I said since about three different people were vying for his attention in our periphery.

He nodded, and we broke apart. I headed toward our table, and Collin turned to pay attention to the person who was standing at his left.

"What was that all about?" Lu asked when I finally got back to the table. "We saw you talking to Collin. You were standing over there forever."

"He asked me out," I said.

"I knew it!" Macy said, pushing at Lu excitedly.

"Don't worry, she didn't say 'yes'," Lu said in a bored, monotone voice.

"How do *you* know what she said?" Macy asked.

Lu looked at me, and I shrugged innocently.

"I told him I don't date."

"What do you mean, you *don't date*?" Macy asked, smirking at me.

"I haven't gone out with anyone since Cameron," I said. "And I don't have plans to."

"She doesn't trust men," Lu added.

"Not even famous ones?" Macy asked.

"That's nothing," Lu said. "She talks to famous people all the time. She's basically best friends with Ethan Prescott."

"We're not best friends," I said.

"They have each other's numbers," Lu said.

Ethan was Dad's biggest-name actor. He had been starring on Bad Medicine for the past five seasons and was a big hit with all the ladies.

"All the actors love her because she's hot and her dad's their boss," Macy said. It was a statement, but I knew she was testing to see if I would deny it.

"Mostly it's my dad," I said, putting away the last two bites of sopapillas they had saved for me. "

I knew by the way Macy and Lu smiled over my shoulder that someone had come to stand behind me. It didn't take a genius to figure out that it was Collin, either. I knew that's who it was before I even turned around. I could barely breathe as I shifted to face him. He smiled and handed me a napkin that was folded in half.

"I wanted you to have it just in case you changed your mind about reaching me," he said.

"Did you ask Sarah out because of her dad?" Macy asked.

Collin pulled back to get a better look at me. "Why do you keep saying that?"

"It wasn't like that, "I said. "I wasn't talking about you. You just came in at the wrong time of the conversation."

He looked at Macy and Lu. "I had no idea who her father was when I tried to get her to go out with me. I asked her out strictly because I was intrigued."

"You called her sunshine," Lu said.

Collin shrugged and smiled. "What can I say? I call it like I see it." He was again whisked away by someone needing his attention, so he patted my shoulder and said, "Thanks again for coming in, ladies," as he walked away with a smile and nod.

My gaze shifted to Macy who was staring at me with an open mouth. "I seriously can't believe you had that guy standing at our table, handing you his number on a napkin."

"We don't even know if that's what's on it," I said, tossing the napkin onto the table.

Macy scooped it up with no hesitation and proceeded to open it and stare at it. "It's his number, all right," she said, placing it back onto the table.

"He just wants to take me out because I don't want to go," I said. "Indifference. It's a wonderful technique. Single women all across the land should use it. I should write a book."

"Unfortunately," Lu said, patting my back with a solid slap. "This one is *actually* indifferent."

"*I'll* go out with him," Macy said, looking around the restaurant as if she might ask Collin if she could take his number since I didn't want it.

"You can have it if you want. I was planning on leaving it," I said. We were done, so we began to gather our things.

Macy squinted at me. "Oh, come on! You can't be serious."

"I am," I said. I shifted my focus to the napkin, considering taking it for a second before looking at her. "I'm not trying to be a man-hater or anything. I love my brothers, and I have a lot of guy friends, but I am not trusting anyone anymore—not like that. It's not that big of a deal."

"It is a big deal," Macy said as she stood, taking the napkin off the table and putting it into her purse. I shot her a curious glance, and she returned it with a shrug. "I'm not gonna to call him. That would just be weird and desperate after he gave you his number and not me. I'm holding onto it for *you* because I think it's a mistake for you to leave it. Plus, I think it's kind of mean. He'll probably pass by here and see that he got rejected."

"He already knows he got rejected," Lu said. "She told him right to his face."

"You guys are making me feel bad," I said. "I thought I was being friendly."

Lu gave me a wink. "You were," she said. "We're just jealous."

Chapter 4

I sent a text to my dad on Nichole's behalf the minute I walked into my apartment. I didn't make a habit of putting a word in for everyone who asked me, but I had looked this girl in the eye and told her I would see what I could do. Plus, in some weird way, I thought helping her out would prove that I wasn't bothered by her getting to go on the set of Best Chef with Collin.

Why am I even contemplating this? I don't even watch cooking shows. I mean, I recognized that guy, but barely. There is absolutely no reason for me to think about him or whatever beautiful waitress he invited to go with him on set.

I typed out the text to my father in spite of (or maybe because of) whatever feelings I was having at the moment.

Me: "Hey, I told a girl I'd mention her name to you. She read for a pilot. Her name's Nichole."

I heard back from my dad instantly. Unless he was working, he was quick to respond to any messages from family. It had been that way since all that legal stuff went down.

Dad: "Is she a friend of yours?"

Me: "Waitress. Just told her I'd mention her name."

Dad: "Okay, honey. We'll see you tomorrow."

Me: "What's tomorrow?"

Dad: "Your brother's birthday dinner."

Me: "Okay, I'll be there."

I included a thumbs up and lightning bolt emoji, and Dad responded with the smiley face with sunglasses. It reminded me of the beach, which sounded delightful considering it was the middle of winter in New York, and I had a particular aversion to being cold. I smiled, thinking about the beach as I threw my phone onto the kitchen counter.

My phone slid, and almost collided with the base of a bowl I had just made. I stared at the results of the brush technique I had done on it, thinking of what I would do differently the next time.

I loved all art, but ceramics were my true passion. I was a better person when my hands were touching clay. The very nature of working with clay was capable of making my perspective shift, and I was thankful everyday that I got to do something I loved.

I sold pieces regularly through consignment, but I didn't make a ton of money at it. In fact, if it weren't for my dad's income, I'd probably be in the same starving-artist situation that Lu, Macy, and Drake were all in (although Drake had been increasingly more successful with his photography in recent months).

I had been working on a project from the time I got home until 6pm when Lu came in the door. She had officially heard from Lane at Shower & Shelter, and she was on cloud nine about her interview, which would take place the following Tuesday.

Lu knew her way around ceramics just from living with me, but her main medium was pen and charcoal on parchment. She worked with watercolor some, too, but most of her art was black and grey. She had a beautiful, whimsical style, and we discussed certain pieces she would take with her to the interview at S&S. We talked about that for a while before I showed her the pieces I had been working on while she was gone.

I didn't look at my phone the whole time I was working, so I had a few texts to answer while Lu chowed down on a box of Chinese noodles she had left over from the night before. She handed it to me when she was done, and I thankfully finished it off since I hadn't even thought about what I was going to do for dinner. I had a television mounted on the living room wall, and I turned it on, sitting cross-legged on the couch with what was left of that box of noodles.

"What channel's Food Network?" I asked, looking over my shoulder at Lu, who was staring down at her phone at the edge of the kitchen.

"I think it's like two-hundred-something, or eight-hundred-something," she said distractedly.

I wrinkled my nose at her even though she wasn't looking at me.

Being the industrious person I was, I visited the preview channel, where I figured out that Food

Network was channel 68. The words "Best Chef" were written all the way across the area where the show titles appeared, indicating that we were in the middle of a Best Chef marathon.

I got nervous and looked over my shoulder as I turned the television to channel 68. Part of me cared if Lu noticed what I was watching, but there was nothing I could do to stop myself from going to that channel—I was just too curious.

"He's not the main guy, you know," Lu said from over my shoulder the instant I changed the channel.

I cringed at getting caught.

"He's not on every episode."

There was a commercial playing, and I tried to hit the fast forward button, but it didn't work.

"You can't do that when it's live," she said.

"I know, it's just habit."

I tossed the remote onto the seat beside me as I continued to eat Lu's noodles. I glanced back at her, wondering if she would comment on the fact that I was leaving it on Food Network, but she didn't. She just stared at her phone again.

***

I ended up watching four episodes of Best Chef in a row. I had never seen it before, and I got hooked. Collin was on the third and fourth episode I watched, making it even more fun.

Lu had gone out not long after I put it on, and she was surprised to find that I was still watching it when she got home. She sat on the couch and finished the last five minutes of the most recent episode with me. I pressed the power button before stretching my arms toward the ceiling.

"Why are you turning it off?" she asked.

"Because that's the last episode of the marathon," I said. "It was an all-new episode. They won't have another one for a week.

"Since when are you a Best Chef expert?" she asked, looking sideways at me.

I giggled and pushed at her. "I was watching it live, remember? All they did during the commercial breaks was pump up the new episode, and we just finished it." I sat back and sighed. "I don't see how they handle all that pressure. There's no way I would want to do that type of thing with pottery where you have a time limit and people stand around and tell me what they did or didn't like about your work."

"It's a good thing there's no cutthroat pottery competition shows out there," Lu said, causing us both to laugh.

"The guy from the restaurant was on that one," Lu added.

"I know," I said. I tried to say it casually, but the truth was, I was painfully aware of that fact that Collin was on that episode. "He was on the one before it, too," I said.

"How many did you watch?"

"Four."

"Oh my gosh, have you been watching it the whole time I was gone?"

"Yeah why?" I asked, a little defensively because of her shocked tone.

"Because, you never watch TV."

"I do sometimes."

"Barely."

"Sometimes I just feel like binge watching," I said.

"Are you sick?"

"No."

"Are you in looove?"

I cracked up laughing at that, but it was a little fake. While it was a completely ridiculous thing to say, her words did strike some sort of weird chord with me. Collin Ross seemed like such a decent person both in his restaurant and on the television. I had been watching him intently for the past two hours, and was wholeheartedly convinced that he was the kindest, smartest man on the planet. He was easy on the eyes, too. I could see how he was so successful on cooking shows in spite of not being a chef. I was compelled to like him.

I flopped over and to the side, burying my head into the couch pillows, and moaning since I felt like a lazy bum for planting my butt in the same position for the past four hours.

"I can't believe you're not denying it," Lu said.

"Denying what?"

"I said you were in love, and you didn't deny it."

I giggled and shook my head without even bothering to sit up or look at her. "I'm not denying it because it's ridiculous," I said. "I thought you were just being silly."

"No, I wasn't," she said. "I know you are because of how you were glued to that show just now."

"I just think it was cool that we met the guy, that's all."

"You meet people who are on TV all the time, Sarah. You can probably run up the street and crash some movie set if you wanted to."

She was right. Not that I ever did it, but I could visit sets of almost any television production I chose. My dad could, no doubt, set up a visit to Best Chef if I asked. I would never ask him to do so, but somewhere in the back of my mind it felt good knowing he could.

"I know, but it's just cool that we met him today, and there happened to be a Best Chef marathon on."

"*It's just cool we met him to day and now there's a marathon on TV,*" she said, repeating my words in a silly way that implied I was lovestruck.

I sat up and hit her with a nearby throw pillow, causing her to laugh and push at me.

"It's a good thing Macy saved that number for you."

"Macy saved that number for herself," I said.

"She did not, and you know it. You should just give in and text him already. I can tell you want to."

I took a deep breath. If ever I would feel tempted to break my own dating rule, it would be with Collin. "It's not that I don't want to call him," I said, feeling confused. I put my hand to my chest. "I think I'm attracted to him."

"Thank goodness!" she said victoriously as if my confession was somehow proof that I was fixed. "I'm attracted to him, but that still doesn't change that I can't call him. I'm not gonna date him."

"Why not?"

"Because," I said in a serious whisper. "Something happened when Cameron did that to me. Something shifted in me. I just can't let my guard down again. It's not even really a choice I'm making, it's more like my body won't even let me do it. I have this push-pull going on inside me where I still like men, and find myself being attracted to them, but I seriously can't think about letting anyone in."

"Not yet," Lu said since she was a glass half-full type of person.

I shrugged. "If I could switch myself back to having hope, I would," I said. "Not that it's all that dramatic," I added. "Lots of people stay single. It's not a big deal."

"*I'm* not staying single," Lu said. "I'm gonna find true love. I'm gonna be working at the gallery one day, and he'll just come walking in off the street. It'll be love at first sight."

"That'll be amazing," I said, grinning at her plan.

Chapter 5

My brother's birthday dinner came and went, and so did several productive days of work where I turned out a few pieces I was really proud of. Lu's interview with S&S went well, although she hadn't heard back from them just yet.

It had been exactly a week since I ran into Collin Ross at his restaurant, and I was happy to report that I had not watched a single minute of Best Chef even though I knew it would be easy for me to access past episodes if I wanted to.

I wasn't watching his show at all, and I did my best not to think of him as days passed, but when Lu asked if I wanted to go out for lunch the following week, I told her I wanted to get Mexican again.

She asked if I wanted to go to the same restaurant we went to the week before, and she didn't give me a hard time about wanting to see Collin when I told her I did—probably because she knew I would deny it and just say I liked the food. We didn't invite Macy or Drake this time since our plans were last minute.

I figured there was only a slim chance Collin would be there, but I still took a little extra care with my hair and makeup just in case. I hated that I wasn't able to keep my heart from beating at a much higher than normal rate as I entered the restaurant with Lu. I told myself to calm down, but it was useless. They were packed, and we had forgotten to make reservations, but the hostess was able to make accommodations for us. She sat us at a small table on the back wall and told us that 'Mike' would be right with us.

I sighed and smiled at Lu from across the table, trying to act like I was excited about the food and running into Collin was not what was on my mind.

"My name is Collin, and I'm gonna be taking care of you ladies today," I heard someone say as he came up beside me.

I must have looked at Lu with a panicked expression, because she began giggling as I turned to see who had spoken. Collin Ross was standing right beside me in all his restaurant owner/food critic glory. He reached in front of me to set down a glass of ice water. "I'll bring lemons if you like," he said.

I looked around, half-expecting for our real server to come walking up behind Collin any second.

He snapped his fingers and made a regretful expression as he said, "I forgot menus. I'll be right back."

Just then, the hostess came rushing up with menus in her hand. She handed them to Collin and they exchanged a smile before he turned to place the paper menus in front of us.

"Sorry about that," he said.

"What are you doing?" I asked, looking around. It felt odd having him serve us, and I didn't know what to make of it.

He smiled, and I stared at his teeth, which had my heart racing again. "I'm taking care of you ladies for lunch," he said.

"He's filling in for Mike," Lu explained as she and Collin swapped smiles.

"Yeah, I'm filling in for Mike," Collin agreed.

"Do you have Mike's other tables?" I asked.

"No ma'am, I don't. Just this one, particular table."

I smiled and glanced down, my heart still pounding. "I'll have some guacamole," I said, hoping my voice would come out steady.

"The chips," he said with another regretful expression. As if on cue, a male server, whom I assumed was Mike, walked up, carrying chips and salsa. Collin took it from him. "Two orders of guacamole for the ladies, please," Collin said.

"Yes sir," the guy said with a nod. He turned to walk away, and Collin placed the chips and salsa in the middle of our table.

He was young and confident, and it was incredibly appealing to hear that well-dressed server call him sir.

"I'm so glad you're here Ms. Spicer. I'm glad you came back. I thought maybe I would have heard from you by now."

I smiled back-and-forth from Lu to Collin, feeling the oddest mix of emotions.

"In the interest of full disclosure, our friend Macy has your number in the front pocket of her purse," Lu said. "She's the keeper of the number. If Sarah ever comes out of her self-inflicted, no-dating phase, we're pretty sure she'll want that napkin."

Collin smiled at Lu and shook his head good-naturedly. "What'd you say your name was?" he asked her.

"Lu."

"Lu," he said tilting his head a little. "Is it short for anything?"

"Lulie."

"Lulie?"

She nodded. "My parents were gonna name me Julie. They called me that when my mom was pregnant with me, and my big sister, who was two at the time, called me Lulie because she couldn't say Julie right. My parents went with it. They named me Lulie, although most people just call me Lu."

"Lulie," Collin said, testing it out as he smiled at her.

Was I jealous? I was jealous. I was flat out jealous. He smiled at her, and my heart sank. I wanted desperately to say something to make Collin look at me instead of my beautiful best friend. I clinched my fists under the table, chastising myself for being so physically swept-away by him. I took a sip of water, moving quickly to mask my shaking hands.

"Take a second to look at the menu. I'll make sure your guacamole comes right out. Lunch is on me today, okay?"

Lu pressed her foot down onto mine with great force when he said he was buying us lunch, and this made me squirm. Collin turned to walk off, and Lu stared at me with wide eyes. Then she squinted and slapped a hand to her forehead. "I can't believe how into you he is," she said as if it pained her to see it.

I laughed and took a bite of a chip to hide how nervous I was. "I can't believe I came here," I said.

"The owner is waiting on us," she said in an amazed voice.

"I bet restaurant owners wait on tables all the time."

"Not ones like him," she said. "How does stuff like this happen to you?"

"Because of my dad," I said.

"Not with him," she said, gesturing in the direction that Collin had gone. "Your dad has nothing to do with that."

"Stop," I said, already feeling anxious and doubting my decision to eat there at all.

"You're the one who wanted to come here," she said, reading my thoughts.

"I know, but I didn't know *he* would be here."

"Don't pretend you came for the food," Lu said, since she knew me too well. "I heard back from S&S," she added. "They said I got the spot."

"You're kidding!" I said with a huge smile.

"When did you find out?"

"This morning."

"Aww, I'm so happy for you," I said.

"There's one catch, though."

"What?"

"It's for a spot that opens up in August. They chose a guy to fill the one coming open next month."

"Why's that a catch?" I asked.

"It means I'm gonna be crashing at your place a little while longer."

"Lu, I really don't mind."

"I know, and I'm thankful, but I know it'll be nice for you to have your apartment back—especially with how my art takes up that whole corner.

"I seriously don't mind," I said.

She smiled at me sincerely. "Thank you for being awesome. You've never asked me for a thing."

"Because I don't want anything from you."

"Sarah, I've been at your place for too long," she said. "I love you for not kicking me out, but it's time for me to kick myself out. I need to make it on my own. S&S is perfect. I'm too comfortable at your place. I've got to get out there and hustle—make it for myself."

"I can appreciate that," I said. "And I'm proud of you. I just want you to know you're always welcome."

She stared straight at me, her brown eyes glazing over like she was holding back tears. "You're awesome," she said.

Just then, a beautiful dish of fresh guacamole landed on our table. I stared at it for a few seconds before looking up at Collin. "The way to a woman's heart..." I said.

He smiled. "I'm trying."

We stared at each other, and I honestly began to feel my heartbeat in the side of my neck because the pounding was so out of control.

Lu cleared her throat. "I'll have the crawfish nachos," she said.

"Good choice." Collin smiled at her and took her menu. "And for you?" he asked, shifting to stare at me.

I cleared my throat since I had heard Lu do it, and I was feeling completely unprepared to speak. "How did you even know what you wanted?" I asked looking at Lu with a confused expression since we had been talking the whole time he was gone.

She shrugged and smiled before taking a bite of chip with a huge pile of guacamole on the end. "It's what I had last time."

"Whatever you think," I said, handing Collin the menu without even looking at it.

His eyebrows drew together. "Anything?" he asked.

"Yep."

"Dietary restrictions?"

"Nope."

"Favorites?"

"Surprises are my favorite."

He was grinning as he turned to head for the kitchen.

"You're in love, you're in love, you're the most in love anyone's ever been in the history of in-loves. You're done for, finished, caput, stick a fork in you."

"You're trippin'," I said, giggling and taking a sip of water since I always got cottonmouth when I was nervous.

"*Surprise me?*" she repeated, staring at me with wide eyes like it was the weirdest thing that could have ever come out of my mouth.

"What? He's the owner. He knows a lot about food. I figured he knew what was good."

"Yeah, but you are not a *surprise me* kind of girl."

"Yes I am."

"Okay, then look me in the eye and tell me you do not like him."

I stared at her for a few seconds. "I can't," I said.

"See?"

"It doesn't mean I'm gonna go out with him."

She chewed her chips as she shook her head in a disappointed manner. "That's just too bad," she said.

"That's your *own* stubbornness causing you to mess with your *own* future happiness."

"Who are you, Dr. Phil or something?"

"I'm the girl who's sitting across from you, watching you and Mr. Right stare at each other like you want to run off and get married."

"We were not." I said, narrowing my eyes playfully at her.

Lu and I went on to talk about other things like the fact that Theo Duval loved her work and told Lane to make a point of saying how excited he was to give her the spot at S&S. The artist compound was a well-oiled machine run by a guy named Lane who had been Theo's right hand in the years when Theo was just starting out. Lane had contacted Lu earlier that morning and reiterated the terms of her room and board at S&S including the guidelines for commissions in the gallery downstairs. Lu was thrilled about the news that she was next in line for a spot, and we talked about that while we waited for our food.

It was about five or ten minutes later when someone else checked in with us. "Mr. Ross wanted me to let you know he had to leave and that I'll be taking care of you from here on out." The guy smiled. "My name's Mike. Mr. Ross has already put in your order, but can I get you anything else?"

I shook my head, feeling disappointed.

Mike smiled. "I'll be back with your food in just a minute. I wanted to introduce myself and let you know I'd be taking care of you. Mr. Ross had to see to an emergency at one of his other restaurants. He was planning on taking care of you, and he apologized for having to step out."

"Oh, it's fine," I said, smiling and trying to seem unfazed. "We weren't expecting him to do that anyway."

Our food came out a few minutes later. It was delicious, and Lu and I were both satisfied with our dining experience, but I was truly sorry that Collin had disappeared during our meal. I kept hoping he would show up before we left, but he didn't.

Mike said lunch was on the house, and we thanked him by leaving a generous tip. We ran into Nichole on our way out. She had gotten a call from my dad's casting director and thanked me for whatever I had done to make that happen. I asked if she had fun on the set of Best Chef with Collin. At first, she seemed surprised that I remembered that, but she said she had an amazing time and even got to taste some of the food.

Moments later, Lu and I headed out onto the crowded sidewalk. We stayed close to the building so neither of us would get trampled by foot traffic. "I'm headed to work," Lu said. She was a barista at a cool little coffee and gelato place. I was tempted to follow her there for some coffee before I went home to get some work done. We hesitated on the sidewalk while I considered my options. I was lost in thought when I heard my name being called from over my shoulder.

Chapter 6

"Sarah," a man's voice called from behind me.

I turned and saw Collin Ross walking toward me with two other people, both men. He had a serious expression on his face, and I wondered what he was thinking and what the emergency must have been. It had taken every ounce of my will not to ask Mike about it when we were in the restaurant.

"Did you ladies enjoy your meal?" he asked.

He came to a stop near us on his way into the restaurant, but it was obvious that he didn't have time to stand there and talk.

"It was soooo good," Lu said.

"It really was," I agreed. "Thank you so much for treating us."

Collin smiled and gave us a curt nod as the hostess opened the door in anticipation of their arrival. I could see the underlying worry in his expression as a result of whatever was going on with his restaurant, and I felt the urge to comfort him. I had to really fight against the desire to reach out and give him a tight hug even though it would have been awkward and completely uncalled-for.

"Maybe I'll see you next week," he said with one last smile and wave aimed at me as they headed into the restaurant.

"I wonder what happened," Lu said.

"I know. Me too."

"Are you coming with me?" she asked.

I was so thrown off by running into Collin that I forgot I had been considering going to get a cup of coffee. I ended up walking with her since it was just a couple of blocks, but I didn't stick around because they were slammed and there wasn't even really a place for me to sit. It was cold outside, so I made quick work of hailing a cab to take me back to my apartment.

We passed Collin's restaurant on our route, and of course, I glanced in that direction. He happened to be standing in plain sight, and traffic was moving slowly, so I watched through the windows for several long seconds as he spoke to a group of people by the door. I stared out of the back window to see him as long as I could, but the traffic had begun to move, and my cab driver continued down the street. Soon, Collin was out of sight, and I turned to face forward again with a sigh.

I worked for a few hours on some number crunching and invoices from the past week's online orders. Paperwork was my least favorite part of the job, so I always saved it up till I absolutely had to pay attention to it. Oh, how I wished I could just make pottery and not worry about selling it. But it that were the case, I'd just have a bunch of stuff sitting on a shelf, never getting used. My father had a trust set up for me, and technically, I didn't have to work, but ultimately it made me feel good.

So, I threw myself into dealing with the business aspect of my art all afternoon. It might have been in an effort to distract myself from Collin, but I was glad to have it done regardless.

The bad part was that my work didn't succeed in making me forget about Collin. I thought about how sweet he had been for wanting to serve us lunch, and how he took time to stop and talk to us at the door even though he was obviously in a hurry. I thought about him saying maybe he'd see me next week, and I experienced a longing feeling in my chest like next week was entirely too long.

Before I knew what was happening, I had picked up my phone and pressed the buttons to call Macy. I held the phone to my ear, realizing how weird it was for me to call her when texting was all we ever did.

"This is Macy," her recording said. "Leave a message after the beep."

"Hey." I paused to clear my throat. "Hey, I was, uh, wondering if you still maybe had that napkin from the other day. This is Sarah. Let me know. Okay, bye."

I cringed as I disconnected the call.

I got a text from Macy a minute later.

Macy: "Sorry, I lost it."

I blinked at the screen, feeling incredibly frustrated at myself for letting her have it in the first place.

Me: "No biggie." I included a smiley face emoji even though I was annoyed. I reminded myself that me not having it was nobody's fault but my own.

Seconds later, a text came through from Macy that said, "JK", along with a clear picture of the napkin.

The level of relief I felt from that text was comical. I might as well have been standing on the edge of a volcano, being made to jump in, and doomed for certain death when someone came up and said, "Stop! Don't make her jump!" That's how relieved I felt. A sense of giddiness washed over me as I stared down at the photo of the napkin with Collin's number written in perfectly legible, plain English. There was no name, but next to the number, there was a simple circle with lines coming off of it in what was clearly the shape of a sun. I literally let out a giggle. I knew there was humor in the 180-degree shift that had happened with my emotions as a result of Macy's conflicting texts.

I text her back with a few emojis, including a praying hand, a thumbs up and a heart, and she responded with a couple of her own.

I took the phone number in the picture, and typed it into a contact that I appropriately named, "Collin." I got to the screen to compose a text to him, but I hesitated since I wasn't sure what I wanted to say.

Me: "Thanks again for lunch today. I just wanted to make sure you were okay."

I stared at my text and ended up deleting the second sentence—the one about making sure he was okay. I left it at; "Thanks again for lunch today," and out of nerves, I pressed send.

I instantly regretted it since I had neglected to tell him who was texting. I typed, "It's Sarah Spicer BTW," and pressed send again, feeling like the biggest dork in the whole world for sending two texts in a row like that.

I tossed my phone onto the couch and flopped down beside it, dreading him texting back almost as much as I dreaded him not texting back.

Nothing.

When I still heard nothing from Collin after five minutes of sitting there waiting for him to reply, I decided to take a shower and get out of the house. My parents had a great apartment right by Central Park, and they always had good food to eat, which was a bonus since I hadn't been grocery shopping in two weeks.

My parents were both home, and my brother, Eli, and his wife, Rebecca, were also there, so it ended up being somewhat of an impromptu family dinner (minus my brother, Joe) featuring pizza from my dad's favorite place down the block.

My parents were both in great moods, and this set the tone for an enjoyable evening. We had a good time, and I was truly enjoying myself. This was why I was completely thrown off when my dad randomly said, "Who's this Collin character?"

I was on the couch and he was standing near the kitchen counter talking to my brother. My head whipped around at the sound of that name, and my dad held up my telephone. "Why are you digging in my phone?" I asked with a warning glare aimed at him.

"I'm not," he defended. "It just flashed across the screen."

He continued by repeating the question, "*Who's this Collin character*," but I barely heard him because I sprang up and over the back of the couch so quickly that it caused my mom, who was sitting next to me, to yelp.

"What'd it say?" I asked, sliding across the kitchen floor with my slippery socks, and almost crashing into my dad as I reached for my phone.

He let out a rumbling laugh, holding my phone just out of my grasp as if he were intrigued by my excitement. "Who's Collin?" he asked, smiling with raised eyebrows.

"Please," I said.

"I thought you were off men," Eli said, teasing me.

"I am," I said, crossing my arms at my father for seriously not giving me the phone. "He's my friend."

My dad handed me the phone with a skeptical grin, and I wrinkled my nose at him. I wanted to act cool and not look at my phone right away, but that was impossible. I pressed the home button as soon as it was in my hand, and here's what I read:

Collin: "You're welcome. My pleasure."

I stared at the screen, feeling the heaviness of disappointment at the brevity of his text.

"Why are you blushing?" Eli asked.

"I'm not," I defended, even though I clearly was. I crossed the kitchen so that my dad and brother would stop looking at me, and I stared at my phone, deciding what, if anything, I should say back.

Before I could text back, I got another text from Collin.

Collin: "Sorry I had to leave."

I smiled, feeling so grateful for the open door to ask about his restaurant.

Me: "Don't be sorry. Mike took excellent care of us. I hope you got things worked out."

Collin: "Glad you enjoyed it. It's been a day for the books. We had a kitchen fire. Things are squared away now. I'll be able to head home soon."

Me: "I'm sorry to hear that. I bet you're tired."

Collin: "I'm always tired. If I'm rested, I'm not working hard enough."

Me: "How about Sunday?"

Collin: "Are you asking me on a date?"

Me: (Smiley face with a tongue sticking out.) "I meant don't you rest on Sundays?"

Collin: "Maybe a little."

I stared at the screen, wondering what I should say next. Sure, I had all sorts of confusing emotions swirling around, but the fact of the matter was that I wanted to see him. *Forget rules or trust issues.* I took a deep breath, staring at the keypad. My heart was beating a thousand miles an hour as I tapped out a response.

Me: "How about Sunday?"

I bit my lip and cringed as I waited for his response.

Collin: "Are you repeating your question, or are you asking me on a date?"

I giggled, which made my whole family look at me.

Me: "I try not to repeat questions."

Bam, bam, bam, went my heart as I pressed send.

Collin: "Sunday's out. I'll be out of town. How about Thursday?"

Me: "Tomorrow?"

Collin: "Yes."

Me: "Yes."

My eyes burned with tears from straight excitement.

Collin: "Send your address and I'll pick you up at 7."

Me: "Dinner?"

Collin: "Yes."

I responded with my address, and he replied back, saying he'd see me the following evening.

Chapter 7

I had seldom experienced the nerves I felt in the hours leading up to my date with Collin. I was at my parents' house when we set up the date, and I got a hard time from my entire family because I couldn't wipe a huge grin off my face for the rest of the evening.

It was now almost time for Collin to pick me up, and I was fit to be tied. I had so much nervous energy that I had cleaned my apartment from top to bottom, shaved my legs, whitened my teeth, and given myself a manicure and pedicure. I had done my very best to prepare myself for Collin's arrival. My apartment was clean, and I was having a good hair day. What could go wrong, right?

Here's what.

At about five minutes till seven, I put on my shoes. I was wearing a pair of black pants, and I wanted to make sure they looked okay together. The shoes had a heel of only a couple inches, and I never had a problem walking in any height heel, but tonight was different. I stepped into the shoes, and somehow, in the three feet of space between myself and the full-length mirror that was hanging in my closet, I managed to roll my ankle painfully to the side.

The fall happened in what seemed like slow motion.

I thought I could catch myself at first, and I let out a yell as I tried in vain to maintain my balance. This was of no use, because the sharp, shooting pain that happened in my ankle made it too difficult for me to bear my own weight. I fell to the side, taking about ten of my dresses along with me and hitting the side of my head on a nearby dresser. I had never in my life done something so clumsy.

What just happened to me? Had I been in that big of a hurry when I was on my way to the mirror?

I made a series of awkward moaning noises as I fell, and before I knew it, I was lying on my closet floor wondering how in the world I ever ended up like that. I had so much adrenaline going that I stood up without really feeling much pain, but it only took a few seconds with weight on my right ankle to realize I was injured.

"Oh my gosh, you have got to be kidding me," I whispered to myself as I hobbled out of my shoes, testing to see if it was any easier to stand without them on.

Pain shot through my right ankle and partially up my leg. I tried to put weight on it, but it felt wobbly, causing me to balance on the other foot. Out of sheer frustration, I groaned and began hanging the dresses I had pulled to the floor with me when I fell. By the time I managed to get them mostly back in their place, the pain in my ankle had really set in.

I was so anxious about my date that you'd think the adrenaline would be enough to get me through, but it wasn't. I flat out could not put weight on my ankle without wincing in pain. The sharp shooting sensation that occurred when I bared down on it could only be lessened by me walking with a limp—and even then, it was difficult.

I was sitting on my couch, staring at my ankle, which I was pretty sure was now swollen when Collin arrived. He rang when he was downstairs, and I hobbled to the door so that I could be there to open it when he arrived.

I was so embarrassed about telling him what happened that just before he knocked on the door, I had myself convinced I could go ahead and fake it and still go on the date. I leaned forward to open the door. Nope. I was wrong. That same sharp pain on the outside of my foot happened whenever I put any significant weight on it.

I did my best to smile and act natural when I opened the door and came face to face with the gorgeous man standing there. Collin. He looked absolutely dashing with fitted jeans and a button-down shirt layered with a wool overcoat.

I hadn't meant for it to be this way, but my expression must have been regretful because the first words out of his mouth were, "You okay?"

I tried to manage a smile even though it was incredibly difficult to ignore the pain and embarrassment I was feeling.

"I don't think I can go anywhere," I said, letting my shoulders slump a little in a defeated way.

"Okayyy," he said, seeing that I was both dressed to go and also melancholy. I could tell he was waiting for me to explain.

"I just did the stupidest thing."

"What?" He stepped inside, and I closed the door behind him. "This is nice," he added, taking in my apartment.

"It's my ankle." I said. There was a devastatingly handsome, wonderful man standing in front of me, and literally, all I could think about was my ankle.

Instantly, a concerned expression hit his face, and he bent to stared down at my legs. I hobbled to the side to let him get a better look. He was kneeling, and he glanced up to look at me when he realized I was having trouble putting weight on it.

"When'd you do this?" he asked.

"Like five minutes ago. Maybe ten. I'm not sure. Just a minute ago."

Collin reached down and, using a hand around the back of my heel, he carefully pulled my foot off the ground so that he could get a better look. I used the wall to steady myself.

"It's swollen," he said, looking up at me with a serious expression.

There was no question in his voice when he made the diagnosis, and the worst went through my mind. "Is it broken?" I asked. I felt a wave of dread wash over me—the kind of wave that had me thinking and feeling the worst. My ears started closing up, and I felt woozy. Before I knew it, I was having trouble focusing on his face, and the next thing I knew, I was seeing spots. I blinked and took a deep breath, trying my best to keep myself together while knowing I was failing at it.

Somewhere in the back of my mind, I had an awareness of crashing onto Collin's chest. Or maybe it was the ground. It was something hard. I felt myself getting jostled, and the next thing I knew, I was blinking up at Collin, who was staring down at me with a worried look on his face. I think I giggled with deliriousness as I came into consciousness again. I experienced a distinct fizzy, bubbly, tingly feeling as I woke up that made me feel ticklish.

"What happened?" I asked, blinking through the delirious haze, and grinning even though I tried not to.

"You passed out," he said.

"I did?" I asked, sitting straight up on the couch, and wondering how I had gotten there. Collin had been leaning over me, but he straightened and took a step back when I bolted upright. I flexed my leg in the process, and when I did, I remembered the cause of my sudden loss of consciousness. My ankle.

"Does swelling mean it's broken?" I asked. I knew it was swollen before Collin even mentioned it, but hearing him say it out loud was what scared me.

He sat beside me on the couch, leaning over to stare at it. "Not necessarily. You can have swelling with a sprain. Did you fall from something?"

I shook my head. "I just rolled it to the side in some shoes. It just happened a minute ago, in the apartment. I feel like the biggest nerd ever. I can't believe I'm having trouble walking on it."

Collin took a seat at my right, and again, he picked up my foot, using a tender approach on the back of my ankle. "I'm sure it's just sprained. My dad's a doctor if you want me to call him, though."

His parents lived in New Hampshire, but within minutes, we were on Facetime with his dad (who was in his robe). He was the sweetest, most down-to-earth man, and after a few questions where he made me stand up and perform certain maneuvers on my foot, he diagnosed me with a sprained ankle. He said it would most likely bruise, and that I should ice it and rest it as much as possible. He mentioned an elastic brace and indorsed a natural product called Arnica. He asked me if I had either of those, and when I said I didn't, he told Collin to run out to the drugstore and buy them. I watched as Collin said goodbye to his dad and then looked at me with a smile.

I was all dressed up to go out, but I was clearly stuck on the couch—Doctor's orders. I let out a long sigh, which made Collin smile. "I'm gonna go get takeout," he said. "I'll pick up Arnica when I'm out. Do you have some icepacks?"

"I have some ice," I said. "But you're not doing all that. I'm fine. I'm just sorry you came all this way and now I can't go anywhere."

"Don't be silly," he said. "I wanted to get takeout anyway. If you want to know the truth, I'm still exhausted from yesterday. This'll be fun."

I stared at him, knowing I should say something to let him off the hook again, but I wanted too badly for him to stay.

"Let me at least call for delivery so you don't have to get out," I said.

He smiled. "I'll go. I can get everything we need within a few blocks. Do you have icepacks?" he asked again.

I shook my head. "Not the official *pack*-packs. I have ice, though."

He gave me another amused grin—one that had me feeling breathless. "I'll go by the drugstore," he said. "What do you want to eat?"

"Anything."

He promised he'd be right back, and I apologized again for our evening not going as planned.

Lu came by while Collin was gone. She knew I was going out, so she was surprised to see me there. She had plans for the evening, and was just coming by to freshen up, so she was gone before Collin ever made it back. I was glad she came home. She helped me hobble to my bedroom so that I could change out of my date clothes and into something more appropriate for being stuck on the couch with a big clubfoot.

Collin rang for me to let him in, and I met him at the door wearing my favorite pair of leggings and an oversized sweatshirt that had a big Indian with feathers on the front. It was my brother's. I think the Indian was some sort of sports logo, but I wore it because I liked the looks of it and it was comfortable and oh so broken-in. I figured if takeout and icepacks were involved, I aught to just go ahead and get comfortable.

Collin was carrying two bags, one paper and one plastic, and he grinned at me as he took in my altered appearance.

"I changed," I said.

His smile widened. "I see that."

"I just didn't want to be stuck on the couch wearing—"

"You look adorable," he said. He stepped past me, kicking his shoes off by the door before heading into the kitchen to set down the bags. "I went for burgers," he said.

"Burgers are perfect."

I limped behind him, heading for the kitchen, but Collin told me to stay behind and park myself on the couch. He made himself at home in my kitchen, cutting our burgers in half and serving them up with French fries and what looked, from where I was sitting, like a salad.

"I got a couple of those gel icepacks, but they're not cold yet, so I also picked up a few bags of peas."

"Peas?"

"It might be mixed vegetables," he said.

"What'd you get that for?"

"For your ankle. I bought the peas since the gel-packs would take a while to freeze."

"I'm totally lost," I said, causing him to stop what he was doing and smile at me.

He held up the bag of frozen vegetables that were sitting on the counter. "I'm gonna put this on your ankle," he explained. "The gel packs are great, but these will get you by until they have a chance to freeze."

"I'm putting peas on my ankle?" I asked.

He grinned. "We're not cooking them first," he said, teasing me. "We're not mashing them up and spreading them on there. You just put the bag on your ankle. The little frozen bits will help it feel better."

I smiled. "Peas, huh?"

"And corn, it looks like."

He crossed the living room and presented me with a perfect plate, which included a side of some specialty dipping sauce. As if that weren't enough, he didn't sit down with his own meal until he had carefully administered Arnica gel and the bag of frozen vegetables to my ankle.

We sat there and ate, talking about sprained ankles and other random injuries we had both endured over the years. He had fallen from a tree when he was a boy and had suffered a broken arm, which left him in a full-arm cast for most of the fifth grade. We laughed as he told the story of how difficult it was to take a bath or go swimming with that huge, cumbersome cast on his arm.

"Tell me something else," I said, after we ate.

Collin had just taken our plates to the kitchen and was on his way back to the living room with a white box in his hands.

"Tell you what?" he asked.

"I don't know," I said.

"Something about yourself."

"I just told you a bunch about myself."

"I know, but something else," I said.

He shrugged. "I hit a deer with my very first car. It happened like the second night I had my driver's license, and I was too embarrassed to tell my parents what happened, so I told them it was a hit and run while my car was parked. Anyway, they found the blood, and called me out on it, so that was pretty embarrassing. My mom had herself all worked up, thinking I had hit a person and left them for dead. Dad said she was already making plans to take me and flee the country."

I giggled, thinking about the sixteen-year-old version of Collin causing so much confusion over hitting a deer, and he laughed along with me.

"Now your turn," he said. I sighed, thinking about what I could or should share with him.

"I was an extra on one of my dad's shows when I was little, and I was so freaked out about doing it that I faked throwing up in the bathroom so that I didn't have to go through with it." I paused and put a hand to my forehead, flinching at the memory. "Oh my gosh, I scooped a handful of toilet water up with my hands so that I could let it fall back into the toilet when I made the gagging noise." I couldn't help but smile at myself for admitting such a thing. "I begged my dad to let me do it, and when it came time, I froze up. I think maybe I was scared I'd fail and disappoint him." I let out a humorless laugh. "I was just an extra. I think I was just supposed to sit at a table and pretend to listen while someone talked to me. Looking back, I was worried for nothing."

"Most worries are for nothing," he said.

"Most are," I agreed. "And sometimes, you're not worried about a single thing, and disaster just swoops right in and blindsides you."

"Sometimes it does," he admitted. "Like when tree branches break when you're sitting on them."

I smiled. "Or when you devastate your ankle by taking two steps in your own closet."

Chapter 8

Collin sat in my living room for the next few hours, but it might as well have been ten seconds with the way it passed so quickly.

We talked about so many things.

He explained his philosophy at work—that he, in a sense, had the mental capacity to provide a quality dining experience for people. It wasn't that he was a great chef or had ever even had the desire to be. He knew how to cook, but mostly he knew how to open and run successful restaurants.

I was able to understand where he was coming from because my dad was the same way with television. He knew the formula, and he was a master at carrying it out. I saw my dad in Collin in some ways, which I both respected and feared.

I wasn't a fool. Collin, much like my dad, was attractive, not only because of his appearance, but also in the confident, capable demeanor in which he carried himself. You can almost tell when a person's smart by just the right sort of eye contact they give you and the way they carry on a conversation, and Collin was smart. His humor was quick and dry, and he had the ability to impersonate people in hilarious ways.

We were laughing at a story he told about having to eat something outrageously gross and pretend to like it so that he wouldn't offend his host when he said, "I better go. I have to be at the airport at five in the morning."

"Oh, I didn't realize your flight was that early," I said, shifting to the edge of the couch so that I could stand up. Between my new brace and the ibuprofen, I was feeling like I could easily limp to the door to tell him goodbye.

"You don't have to get up," he said, seeing me move. "In fact, I could help you to your bed if you want me to."

My perv-o-meter was so sensitive, that I gave him a skeptical glance when he said, "bed" even though he didn't mean anything by it. I had been pretty candid with Collin during the last few hours. I had shared my experiences with men, and I could tell he noticed me take his offer the wrong way. He shifted on the couch so that our knees were almost touching and we were mostly facing each other. We hadn't had any physical contact other than him touching my ankle, but at this point, he reached out and put his hand on my knee. I stared at it for a second before making eye contact with him, my heart feeling like it might go beating right out of my chest. His hand was warm. I could easily feel the temperature of it through the thin fabric of my leggings. I had to remind myself to breathe.

And yet, somehow in the midst of all that, I knew something had shut down inside of me. In spite of my crazy physical reaction to Collin, I still knew I wasn't capable of fully trusting anyone.

"What?" he asked, taking his hand from my knee, only to run his fingertips along the side of my face.

"Nothing," I said, smiling at him and feeling, for some reason, like I wanted to cry.

He dropped his hand, resting it again on my knee. "Listen, Sarah, I'm not gonna say you're wrong about men being despicable creatures, because we are. I won't say I'm perfect, because I'm not. I have been in relationships and felt myself being attracted to women who were not the person I was dating. I had to make a choice not to follow-through on my thoughts. Everybody feels temptation at sometime or another—not just men. I'm not saying you're wrong for having trust issues, but at the same time, you should know that there are people out there who can refrain from following every little urge they have."

I smirked at him. "You wouldn't happen to know one of those people, would you?"

"You're one," he said, even though he knew I was fishing for him to say *he* was one.

I nodded. "You're right," I said. "I think exclusivity is hot. It's powerful. I watched my dad lose respect when he did what he did, and I'm not willing to do that. My ex's, too. That's exactly why I'm so glad I've chosen to wait."

Collin took a deep breath and rubbed his eyebrows as if gathering his thoughts. He kept his eyes closed when he said, "Seriously, Sarah."

"Seriously, what?"

He stared at me, shaking his head imperceptibly. "You've said the word 'wait' a couple of times when we were talking, and now you said it again. Are you referring to waiting till you get married? Is that what you're talking about?"

I felt blood rush to my face at his words. Not knowing whether this was a turn-off or a turn-on, I settled for making a *where are your manners* face at him like I didn't want to answer.

This made him smile. "Is it? Are you?" he asked sweetly.

I nodded shyly. "That's the whole point of them cheating on me."

He reached out to take my hand. "Sarah," he said. I was staring down, but I glanced at him when he said my name. He just sat there and stared at me for a few seconds in silence. He took a deep breath, wearing an expression that said he was carefully trying to consider his words. "I, uh, don't even know where to begin to tell you how that makes me feel. I don't think *I* even know how it makes me feel." He glanced down again, searching for the right words. "I feel like I should hoist you over my shoulder and drag you off to the wilderness and marry you, or something."

I giggled since I had not, by any stretch of the imagination, expected him to say that. "The wilderness?" I asked, laughing.

He scooted toward me, till our knees were pressed against each other. This put us in such close proximity that I could smell him—feel his energy. My eyes roamed over his face, noticing the way the shadow from a nearby lamp fell on the hollow of his cheek.

"Sarah, I really am sorry for what those other men have chosen to do in your life." He paused. "Maybe I'm not really that sorry, if I'm being honest, because if they hadn't, then you might not..." he trailed off, sighing and smiling at me. "I just think you should know that commitment is commitment in my book. And I know about discipline. Quite frankly, you can't get to where I am in business without becoming a master of those two attributes."

"Are you saying it would take discipline to refrain from cheating on me?" I asked. "How romantic."

He gave me an amused grin as he shook his head. "I'm saying that staying true to one person in a relationship takes discipline. Maybe not at first, and maybe it's harder for some people than others, but temptation comes to everyone." He paused and scanned my face. "I really can't imagine ever doing anything to hurt you, Sarah," he said, sincerely. "It honestly baffles me to think about having you and throwing it all away. What sort of idiots were you dating?"

I smiled, taking his hand into both of mine as I wiggled my shoulders a little. "You're leaving," I said.

"Yep."

"For how long?" I asked, even though I already knew the answer.

"It'll be a month, but remember, I'll fly in for a day on my way to London."

We sat there, unblinking.

"Can I see you?" he asked. "When I come home for a day?"

I nodded, which was an understatement to the intensity of my agreement. *How was it that a week ago he was barely on my mind, and now I felt desperate for the next time I'd get to see him?*

"I think it's the first weekend of March, but I'll let you know."

I nodded again.

He stood up, straightening his clothes and stretching. "I better get going," he said regretfully.

I stood, and he caught me in his arms. "You don't have to get up," he said, staring down at me as he supported some of my weight with a hand around my back.

I wanted so badly to stay wrapped in his arms that I stood there in silence when I should have been responding to what he had said. In fact, I didn't even remember what he said or care if the silence was awkward. In a gesture of relaxation, I sighed and placed my forehead on his chest as I shifted my weight to balance on my good ankle.

Collin rubbed my back. "I'm sorry, not sorry they hurt you, Sarah," he whispered.

I breathed a little laugh. "I'm sorry about all the walls," I said, knowing any other girl would be throwing herself at him by this point.

He ran his hand over my back, and I breathed in his clean, masculine smell. "They don't say patience is a virtue for nothing," he said, patting my back in a way that made me know he was preparing to leave. "I'm one of the most patient people I know." He was clearly saying he would wait some undisclosed amount of time for me, which was hard for me to believe even though it was vague.

"I know about temptation," I blurted.

Collin had already turned as he was preparing to leave, but he looked at me when I made that off-the-wall statement.

"I understand what it's like to be drawn to someone… physically."

He tilted his head at me as if interested to hear how I'd continue.

"Okay, the side of me that's been hurt wants to tell you I can never see you again, meanwhile, I'm screaming at myself to reach out and touch your face—to make you kiss me."

"I can assure you, Miss Spicer, there would be no *making me* about it," he said jovially.

I pulled away, and Collin crossed to the kitchen to get his coat. He carried it with him to the living room before putting it on, and I limped with him to the door. He offered to help me, but I told him I could manage. It hurt with every step, but I had enough adrenaline going to ignore it.

"I had so much fun," I said as we got to the door. It was the understatement of the century. I was more comfortable with Collin than I had ever been with anyone in my whole life, even Lu. It didn't matter that I barely even knew him. I trusted him and loved him innately.

"Listen, Sarah, if there's even a chance that you're thinking about liking me, then I'm gonna wait for you. I'm not gonna see anybody else if you think something could ever..."

"Are you alive?" I whispered, staring at his irresistible face.

He smiled and touched his own jugular vein as if checking to make sure before he bent to put on his shoes. "I'm not the same as you, Sarah. I wish I could say I was, but I'm not, and it is what it is. I can't change my past, but I can tell you, I will wait for you if you say there's a 'yes' somewhere down the line."

Breathe. In for four seconds, hold for four seconds, out for four seconds.

"Is that a 'no'?" he asked.

"No," I said defensively. "Why do you say that?"

"Because you're not saying anything."

"Because I'm trying to say the right thing," I said honestly.

He smiled. "I pretty much know you like me," he said confidently. "I just wanted to hear you say it, I guess."

"I do like you," I said, knowing I shouldn't deny it even though the thought to do so had crossed my mind.

"Okay, so I'm going to Chicago, and then home for a day, and then to London, and I'm not looking at other girls, because there's one back here at home who'll be waiting for me, right?"

His words sent jolts of electricity shooting through my abdomen, but he just stared at me with a deadpan, no-nonsense expression. I smiled and covered my face with my hands, feeling shy, like he might somehow see how much I liked him just by the look on my face.

"I thought we get to say 'hi' between Chicago and London," I said, avoiding his actual question, which had me feeling breathless.

"We will..." he said, waiting patiently for me to say more.

"And I think I would like it very much if you didn't worry about checking out other girls while you're gone," I added in little more than a whisper. I bit at the inside of my mouth, and flinched as I listened to hear what he'd say.

He stepped closer to me, invading my space to the point where our bodies were almost touching, and he leaned down to speak near my ear. "That guy you've been saving yourself for?"

"Uh-huh?" I asked, wanting so badly for him to continue.

"That's me."

Chapter 9

Collin Ross did not, I repeat, did *not* kiss me that night. We had done a lot of talking about my trust issues, and he was obviously being respectful. I could tell he wanted to do it, and it was difficult to keep myself from encouraging him, but I knew it was best to take our foot off the gas a little bit.

He wasn't chipping away at my carefully constructed walls; he came at me like a wrecking ball. I could feel my inhibitions crumbling to bits when he looked at me, and I knew I could easily get swept away and wind up hurt again. I was relieved in some ways that he had a trip planned so that I could take a step back and figure out how I was feeling.

Collin called me the first night he was gone, and we ended up talking on the phone for about an hour. This continued for the next eight days until he flew home to regroup for his trip to London. We had talked about so much in our phone conversations, that I felt like the Collin I would see tonight was an entirely different person from the one I had been with a week before.

I knew so much about him now. I respected his hustle and determination. I knew his likes and dislikes. I knew what inspired him, and what his goals were. I even knew what to get him for his birthday (which would take place while he was still in London). I decided I'd give it to him early since he would be gone for the occasion. I knew where he'd be staying in London, and I could have easily shipped it to him, but I simply wanted to give it to him early. It was something I knew would look good on him, and part of me wanted to give it to him for selfish reasons so that I could see him wearing it.

Collin's flight was to land in New York at 1pm, and he said he needed the afternoon to see to a few matters with his restaurants. I was to meet him for dinner at one of his restaurants named The Blue Inn. He would send a driver who would be at my house at 6. I had been to this particular restaurant and really enjoyed it (not knowing it was Collin's at the time).

My ankle was still slightly unstable, but it had come a long way since it first happened. What an ordeal that was. I could barely walk on it for the first three days. Thankfully, I was much better now, and was finally back into my normal shoes.

***

It was a Saturday evening, and the streets and restaurant were packed. The hostess introduced herself as Danielle and took my coat before showing me to a table for two in the back of the dining room.

"Mr. Ross is just finishing up in the kitchen," she said with a smile. "He'll be out in just a moment. Your server will be right over to take care of you. Can I get you anything until then?"

I shook my head and smiled at her as I settled into my chair, and she was off without another word.

Collin came out of the kitchen before the server got to me. I saw him right when he came around the corner, and I could hardly remember to breathe. He was clean-shaven, and his hair was combed away from his face. He was wearing dark, fitted clothes—black slacks and a button down shirt with subtle stripes. I had to glance away to contain my nerves. By the time I looked at him again, I noticed that some customers had stopped him, and he was now engaged in conversation with them.

The server came over with an appetizer and our drinks. He introduced himself as Neil and said Collin had already ordered our food while he was in the kitchen and that he would be right over. Neil had just walked away when I turned to Collin. Within seconds of looking his way, he glanced back at me. His gaze was fleeting, but when he noticed that I was staring back at him, he did a double take and smiled. I smiled back, and I took great pleasure in watching him have to peel his eyes off of me so that he could focus on wrapping up the conversation with the people sitting at the table.

He said something to them before pointing straight at me. All four of them looked in my direction, and I smiled and gave them a little wave, causing them to all wave back. Collin said a few more words to them before clapping his hand on the closest gentleman's back.

He began walking toward me with an expression that said he wasn't going to stop until he made it there. I giggled at his look of determination, feeling giddy that his attention was focused on me even though every table in the place would have loved to have him stop and talk to them.

I could hardly get a good breath of air into my lungs. I stood up when Collin was a few feet away, and he stopped walking, looking me over. He took the last step, wrapping his arms around me to draw me in for a hug.

"How's my girl?" he asked.

"Good."

"How's the bum ankle?"

I pulled back and smiled. "Not quite normal, but better."

He grinned at me, and my heart leapt. "If I had more time, I would have taken you to a restaurant that wasn't mine."

"I love coming to your restaurants," I said. "I like seeing you in your element."

"I'm glad, but just so you know, it's likely we're gonna be interrupted."

"That's fine," I said.

"Probably more than once," he said. He reached down to place a kiss on my cheek before taking a seat at our table. "I'm sorry it's such a rushed stay this time," he added. "I planned it as a work layover. That was before I knew you."

"I don't want you to feel like you have to sit here and have a meal if you need to work," I said.

He leaned back in his chair, grinning at me with his glorious mischievous grin. "I have been looking forward to this moment for over a week," he said with a relieved sigh. Collin was so down to earth and approachable which was in contrast to his tailored, carefully thought out style. He used his hands to wipe his face before focusing on me again. "I'm so happy to see you. I have about two or three hours of work to do at other restaurants tonight, and all I want to do is sit on the couch with you sitting next to me in your Hawks shirt."

"What's a Hawks shirt?" I asked, making him laugh.

"Your sweatshirt with the Indian," he said. "It's the logo for the Blackhawks. They're a hockey team."

"Why don't we have dinner, and then maybe I could tag along while you finish work. We can do some couch-sitting after that."

He sat up in his chair and leaned across the table, looking relieved to see me. This put me in the best mood.

"I would *love it* if you hung out while I finished up," he said, seeming thankful that I would offer such a thing.

"You can put me to work if you need to, or I could just stay out of your way. Whatever would help."

Collin and I ate the appetizer, and just as we were finishing, the second course came out, and then a third, and forth. Neither of us ever ordered anything. Collin must have taken care of all that ahead of time.

The server had just brought us dessert and coffee when I decided to give Collin his birthday present. I wanted to give it to him the minute I saw him, but I had been so breathless that I figured I'd give myself a little time to calm down. We had begun talking about his trip and the restaurant he was visiting in Chicago, so it slipped my mind to give it to him until we were nearing the end of our meal.

I pulled the rectangular jewelry box out of my clutch and slid it across the table toward him. It was the perfect gold chain for his perfect neck. It wasn't too thin or too thick, and if my dad's jeweler was good at his job, which he was, it should rest perfectly atop Collin's collarbones, at the base of his neck.

I was going out on a limb by giving it to him, but I knew he didn't have one, and I also knew it would look amazing on him. He gave me a sideways glance when I slid the box toward him.

"I have a card, but it wouldn't fit in my purse, and I got a little embarrassed to carry it in. It's at my house."

"Did you write in it?" he asked, not letting me break eye contact as he put his hand on mine to take the gift I was offering.

"I wrote a big, long heartfelt paragraph," I said. "You woulda been touched."

I giggled, doing my best to regulate my breathing, trying to absentmindedly count to four without actually counting.

"What'd it say?" he asked. He slid the box out from under my hand, pulling it across the table toward himself.

I suddenly regretted getting something so personal when we were still new at this. "Never mind," I said, putting my hand on the box as if I was about to take it back. He gave me a dubious glance before easily sliding it out of my grasp, holding it to his chest with an expression that said he dared me to take it away. He knew I wouldn't cause a scene in his restaurant, so he smiled and lifted his eyebrows at me as he unwrapped the silver paper from the box and opened it. He glanced inside and then up at me.

"Is it a necklace?" he asked.

I nodded. "I noticed you don't wear one," I said. "I thought it'd look good on you, but if you don't wear them for some reason, and you can't use it, you can just take it back. It's my dad's jeweler, so he'll be cool with—"

Collin cut me off. "I love it," he said. "I'm not giving it back."

I watched as he took it out of the box and tested the weight of it in his fingers. "It's perfect," he said.

"I know," I said, staring at the place where it would fall, which I could see past the collar of his shirt.

"You're gonna have to put this on me," he said.

I nodded.

He carefully placed the necklace back in the box. "We'll do it on the way to our next stop," he said. "I love it. My dad didn't wear any jewelry because he was always having to scrub up for surgery. I've never been much of a jewelry guy. I really didn't know I would like something like that, but I'm stoked to try it on. Seriously, thank you."

Collin and I wrapped up our dinner, and before I knew it, we were headed to another restaurant a few miles away. It would take us about thirty minutes to get there, and the best part of it all was that I got to ride with Collin in the backseat. One of the first things we did was put on his necklace. He handed me the box, and turned away from me so that I could fasten it for him. I easily handled the clasp, dropping it into his collar once it was secure. He turned to face me as he reached up to adjust it. Dad's jeweler was a genius. The gold chain I bought him peeked out of his dark shirt, falling at the perfect place, just below that indention in his neck. I sighed blissfully as I stared at it.

He laughed and touched it as he relaxed into his seat. "It's heavy," he said as a compliment.

I smiled and wiggled my eyebrows.

"How does it look?" he asked.

"Amazing," I said with a smile.

"It's possessive, you know."

I puled back, leveling him with a curious expression.

"It is," he said, shrugging one shoulder.

"What's that mean?" I asked.

"Jewelry," he said, glancing down at it again even though he couldn't see it past his chin. "It's a possessive gift, don't you think?"

"I *didn't* until you said that," I said.

He stretched out comfortably like he was the king of the backseat. "I think it means you're into me," he said.

"Oh yeah?"

"Yeah. I'm pretty sure of it. Are you gonna enjoy knowing I'm wearing it while I'm in London?" he asked.

I thought about being vague, but I went for honesty. "Yes, actually," I said. "I hope you do wear it." I leaned forward so that I could get a good look at the necklace, and before I could stop myself, I reached out to touch it. I let my fingertips fall on it, trying not to be affected by the warmth of Collin's neck. "Is that possessive of me?" I asked.

"I hope it is," he said.

"What are you gonna say if someone asks you where you got it?" I asked.

"They won't."

"What if they do?"

"What did you tell the jeweler?" he asked, turning my question around. "Who'd you say you were getting it for?"

I was speechless for a few seconds, because I had actually mentioned that it was for my boyfriend since I figured it'd be weird to buy a nice piece of jewelry for anyone else.

"What?" I asked, avoiding his question.

"Who'd you say it was for?" he asked.

"You," I said.

Chapter 10

"I'm sorry it's such a quick trip," Collin said, glancing out the window of the car. We were fairly close to his restaurant, but traffic was terrible, a fact for which I was grateful since it kept me cooped up in the car with him these last extra minutes.

He flopped his head onto the headrest with a tired sigh. His eyes were closed, but he smiled sweetly since he knew I was looking at him.

"Tired?" I asked.

"So tired," he moaned, still smiling a little. I sat there and stared at his cheekbone—how the lights fell on it. Feeling like I wanted to comfort him in some way, I leaned forward and placed a kiss right on the spot I'd been staring at. His smile broadened, although he still didn't open his eyes. I leaned forward and did it again, this time allowing my lips to remain on his cheek for two, three, four seconds. A warm sensation washed over me, causing me to curl my toes and clinch my fists. I broke contact, and this time, instead of keeping his eyes closed, he peeked at me with one eye.

I giggled.

"I'm gonna try this again," he said.

Again, he rested his head on the seat back and stared upward, closing his eyes and not paying attention to me at all. I stared at the side of his face for a few seconds before falling into his trap. I leaned over and placed my mouth on his cheek again. This time I went for the soft spot, right in the center of his cheek, closer to his mouth. I barely had the chance to touch his cheek when he turned, forcing our mouths to make contact.

I was so looking forward to this moment.

I loved his whole face—but especially his mouth. I had been checking him out on reruns of Best Chef, and I just loved the way he looked. I had imagined kissing his perfectly curved mouth, and now, at this very moment, it was happening. Without taking his lips from mine, Collin shifted so that we were facing each other more fully. Our lips connected with such a delicate touch, that subtle movements from the car would make us lose contact for a split-second. He leaned in and kissed me more firmly once, and then again before pulling back to stare at me. His light eyes roamed over my face. I had no idea what he was thinking. He smiled before kissing me again. Three times, he let his lips touch mine, and just like that, we were pulling to a stop in front of his restaurant.

I was so shaken up by his kiss that it felt like I was dreaming when Collin withdrew and whispered, "We're here."

I smiled, and glanced out of the corner of my eye before staring at him again. "We're here," I repeated since my thinking skills had turned to goo the second he kissed me.

"I have a couple hours of stuff to do in here," he said as we walked into the restaurant. This was another Mexican restaurant, although it was even more upscale than the one where I first met him.

"I'll just stay out of your way unless you can find something for me to do," I said. "I think I'll start with a visit to the ladies room, though."

He smiled and pointed toward a hallway on the far side of the dining room. "The restrooms are back there," he said. "I have some stuff to deal with in the kitchen and then I'm meeting with my executive chef."

"Go," I said. "Do what you need to do. I'll keep myself busy. I might go for a walk or something."

Collin smiled and squeezed my arm as if saying thanks for understanding as he took off for what I assumed was the kitchen. I glanced at his neck as he turned, and smiled, loving the sight of my necklace on him.

I heard someone say my name when I was on my way to the ladies room. "Sarah Spicer?" A woman's voice came from my right, and I turned to find an actress from one of my dad's shows named Barbara Long. She was with about eight people at a booth along the wall, and I walked over there to greet them. "Sarah is Saul Spicer's daughter," she explained as I got closer.

"I know Sarah," a guy said.

I turned to find her assistant, who I recognized from the set. I waved at him.

"Sarah went to Columbia for pottery," he said proudly to the others at the table. I didn't correct him even though that wasn't entirely true since what I earned was more of a general art degree.

"I've seen her stuff," Barbara said. "Her dad has a few of her things in his office." She cocked her head at me and stared at me seriously as if something had just dawned on her. "I should probably buy a couple of your little bowls," she said. "I have to get my agent something for his birthday, and he loves all that homemade stuff."

I smiled as graciously as I could even though she was implying that my ceramics were some type of hobby or craft project. Oh well, I thought, so goes the life of an artist. Drake had taken some portraits of me in my studio, and I had business cards made with my favorite one. I happened to have one of them in my purse, so I took it out and put it on the table in front of Barbara.

"I have an online store if you want to check out some of my work."

"She's really good," Skip, the assistant said, reaching for my card. "She went to Columbia."

I smiled and waved at them, "It was great seeing you guys," I said.

"You too, sweetheart," Barbara said.

I bowed at them as I turned and continued through the dining room to the women's restroom.

There was a small dressing area with a couple of couches, and I stayed in there for nearly a half-hour after I used the restroom. The restaurant was busy, but nobody was hanging out in the women's restroom, so aside from the people passing by on their way to and from, I was alone. I had a few texts from Lu and my mom, so I took care of those before spacing out on the internet for a while.

I thought I might sit at the bar for a while or maybe even walk to the bookstore down the street. I made up my mind to go to the bookstore since Collin said he might be a couple of hours. I had just come out of the restroom and was about to round the corner that led to the dining room when I saw Collin standing on the other side of the restaurant with his back toward me.

I knew it was Collin by what he was wearing and how he was standing. I knew it was him. It was Collin; that was all there was to it. That fact wouldn't have been so hard for me to believe had there not been a blonde standing beside him with her arms wrapped around his waist like she was a freaking koala bear. I mean seriously, she was holding onto him with a unashamed grip around his middle.

Just then, someone came into the hallway, and not seeing I was standing there, they almost bumped into me. We both gasped and giggled at the awkward encounter, but soon, she was off to the ladies room, and I was once again, staring at Collin's backside. The girl's dad-blasted arms were *still* wrapped around his middle. I stepped to the side so that I could see Collin without being in anyone's way. I knew I should walk away and not watch what was happening, but when you're in a position like that, it's literally impossible. I stood there and watched them like a little kid playing spies. The woman had obviously been at one of the tables, and stood up to hug him when he went to talk to them. A hug was one thing, but she just kept her arms wrapped around him while he talked to the others at the table.

I thought about how long I had been in the ladies room, and it came to me that Collin probably thought I had gone on a walk like I said. He apparently had no idea I was still in the building, or he would clearly not be doing this. My heart felt heavy and out-of-joint like the center of my chest had hiccupped and my heart was now slightly out of place. I closed my eyes and let out a hopeless sigh.

I blinked, hoping against hope that I had been dreaming and the blonde by his side would be gone when I looked up, but I had no such luck. They stood there, continuing to talk and laugh. I had the pleasure of watching as Collin lovingly patted her waist and leaned down so that she could place a kiss on his cheek. Someone walked by me right when the kiss happened, and I gasped at being startled.

"Sorry," the guy said since he hadn't seen me.

I smiled. "Oh, it's my fault. I wasn't paying attention to where I was going."

I was giving him false information he didn't even need, but I had to babble because my only other alternative would be to burst out crying. One more glance in Collin's direction, and I saw that he was smiling and waving to everyone at the table as he headed back toward the kitchen.

I waited until he was out of sight, and then I made my way to the front door. I moved as quickly as I could without drawing attention to myself. I heard someone say my last name while I was on my way, but I acted like I missed it completely. I had one thing on my mind, and that was getting out of that restaurant and as far away from Collin Ross as possible.

I didn't even realize how cold it was. My heart was pounding and hot blood coursed through my body as I navigated the sidewalk toward the bookstore. I was about halfway there when I realized there was no reason for me to go to the bookstore at all.

I stopped to hail a cab and was thankful that one saw me right away. I told the driver my address and rested my head on the seatback, unable to get the vision of Collin with the blonde out of my head. I tried to tell myself it was his sister, but I knew that wasn't the case, because she was married with kids and lived in New Hampshire right down the road from his parents. Plus, I had seen her picture, and she was not blonde.

I tried to tell myself it could have just been a friend or fan of his, but the familiar way she held onto him stuck in my head. There was just no denying it—the blonde in the restaurant was showing him affection, and he was returning it. Maybe this shouldn't be such a terrible thing—I mean it's not like he stood there and made out with her or anything. But he showed her affection, and I just wasn't the type of girl who was secure enough to watch him do that.

I tried to tell myself it wasn't a big deal, but I just kept seeing the scene over and over again with her arms wrapped around his middle. Way too familiar. She was pretty, too, at least what I could see of her from where I was standing.

Lights and the sights of the city flashed past me as I rode home in the cab, but I didn't really see any of it.

Chapter 11

I was completely out of it the whole way to my apartment. It was freezing, and it had begun to sleet, which added to the haziness of it all.

I felt sick.

My cab ride lasted the better part of an hour. It took even longer than it should have because the driver made a wrong turn, and even then, I was too out-of-it to care. In my ponderings, I decided that even if, by some chance, there had been a misunderstanding, there was still something wrong with my reaction to seeing him with that woman. I had seen enough movies and read enough books in my life to know that misunderstandings like this happened, but I just couldn't live this scared, this skeptical, this paranoid. Even if there was nothing going on between Collin and that blonde, I couldn't go on getting broken hearted every time I saw him hug one of his customers.

I went through the motions of greeting my doorman, but I was glad for the sleet so that I could walk past him in a hurry. In a blur, I unlocked my apartment, tossed my coat onto the catchall, and crossed the living room where I collapsed onto the couch. My phone was in the back pocket of my pants, and I shifted so that I could take it out and set it on the coffee table. I knew I had to contact Collin, but I was still undecided as to what I'd say. It took me a few minutes of grasping for as much logic and reason as I could to decide to be as vague and gracious as possible. I made a specific effort to be unemotional as I typed out a text to him.

Me: "Hey, I went ahead and came home. I'm not feeling my best, and I know you have a lot to do. We'll hook up when you get back from London. You'll be missed. Thanks again for dinner, I had fun."

It was a long text, but I didn't want to take any of it out. I thought it was necessary to put things about missing him and hooking up again later because we had already grown too close for me not to acknowledge that I'd miss him.

My heart fluttered as I pressed send, and I sat there reading the text I had just written two or three more times. I watched my phone for about a minute, but when he didn't text me back within that time, I went into my bedroom.

I turned on the television for background noise and took a shower. I was almost certain Lu wouldn't be home soon, but either way, I kept my bedroom door closed so I wouldn't be disturbed.

I had just gotten out of the shower and was channel surfing when my phone rang. I gasped before I leaned over to grab my phone. I stared at the screen, which clearly told me there was an incoming call from Collin.

I sat there and held the phone in my hand, feeling like too much of a coward to pick it up. I didn't want to press decline, so I just held the phone until it stopped ringing, which seemed like an eternity.

My heart raced as I waited to see if he'd leave a message. I was staring at my phone when a text message popped up on my screen.

Collin: "Are you here?"

Obviously, he thought I was still waiting for him at his restaurant. I knew if I didn't text him back that I ran the risk of him coming over here, which I did not want. I had already wasted enough of Collin's time on a day that didn't have enough hours.

Me: "Did you get my text? I'm here at my apartment. Sorry I missed your call just now. I'm not feeling good and decided to come home."

I pressed send, and within seconds, I heard back from him.

Collin: "I'll be done in an hour. I'm sorry you're sick. Can I bring you something? I hope it wasn't the food."

Me: "No, it's not the food. I think it's allergies. It works out. I know you have to wake up early to catch your flight. Thanks again for tonight!" I included a kissy face emoji because I knew it'd be suspicious if I quit cold turkey on little sentiments like that.

Collin: "I wish I could see you before I go. I'm almost done here."

Me: "I think I'm gonna hit the sack."

Collin: "Pick up your phone."

Within seconds, my phone was vibrating. It all happened so fast that I let out a little screech and tossed my phone onto the bed next to me as if it were a hot potato. But I knew I had to answer the call, so just as quick as I tossed it down, I picked it up again, pressing the button to answer the call.

"Heyyy," I said, trying to sound groggy.

"You okay?" he asked.

"Yeah, I, just, I knew you had a lot of work to do tonight, and it worked out because I was sort of tired and under the weather. I think it's the sleet making my allergies flare up."

I clinched my fist and pinched my eyes shut, telling myself to be quiet and stop giving him too much information. I could hear the hustle and bustle of the restaurant around him, and I felt sick that he was taking time out of his night to worry about me.

"The thing that helps me when I get like this is sleep, so I'm gonna go ahead and hit the sack," I said, groggily.

"Sarah, be straight with me," Collin said in an impassive tone. "What's going on?"

"I don't want to see you," I said honestly after a few seconds hesitation.

"Did I do something?"

"No, you didn't," I said. "It's me."

"The old, *it's not you, it's me,* thing?" he asked. "Is that what you're doing?"

"Yeah, but it really *is* me," I said.

"So, you just changed your mind about being with me," he asked.

"I wasn't with you," I said. "We're not…" I trailed off.

"We're not what, Sarah?"

"We're not a thing."

Collin breathed a humorless laugh. "Seriously?" he asked.

My heart pounded and ached at the same time. My chest was a chaotic mess.

"It's my fault," I said. "It's the trust stuff. I should be able to see some girl's arms around you and be cool and confident with that, but I can't. It's me, not you, just like I said." I started to hang up after I said that, but I caught myself, and instead waited to see what he would say.

"What are you talking about?" he asked.

"The blonde."

"My little cousin?" he asked. "At the table in the corner? Elaina. She just turned eighteen, and she wants to start working at one of my restaurants."

There was a short silence.

"I honestly knew in the back of my mind it was probably some kind of misunderstanding," I said. "I had already considered that. But the point is that I'm still afraid, Collin. It's the trust thing. It's something I need to work on—something I have to figure out for myself. I don't want to drag you into it."

"You have to forgive them, Sarah—all those men in your life who made wrong choices—all the women, too, for that matter—everyone who wrongs you. You have to forgive them. I heard one time that unforgiveness is like drinking rat poison and waiting for the rat to die. You're wishing harm, or at least justice, on the person who wrongs you, but all that's happening is *you're* stuck remembering it. You're the one drinking the poison."

I had never heard that before, and I did my best to let his analogy sink in, even though it all still felt a bit like I was in a dream and it didn't really apply.

"You have to forgive people, Sarah, or you'll never be able to trust."

"That's exactly what I'm telling you," I said (even though I was sure he was saying it much better than I was). "I'm not able to trust, and I don't want to drag you into that."

"Too late. I'm already drug," he said.

Instantly, an ember of joy and hope to begin bubbling somewhere deep inside me.

"I have to go," he said. "Please reconsider and let me come by on my way home, Sarah. I really want to see you before I leave for London."

"Okay," I said.

"Okay," he agreed. "I'll be here for roughly another hour. I'll call when I'm on my way."

"Okay," I said. "See you soon."

"See you in a bit," he said, in a way that meant goodbye. He was already talking to someone else as he hung up the phone with me, and I heard them telling him something about a shipment of fish. I hung up the phone and held it to my chest, feeling overjoyed about learning the identity of the mystery blonde, and utterly gobsmacked at the fact that Collin was coming over when I seriously had myself convinced I would never see him again. I stared at the ceiling of my bedroom, thinking about that rat poison analogy and wondering if I had truly forgiven the people in my life who had hurt me. I thought I had forgiven them, but maybe I hadn't.

I squeezed my eyes closed and said a prayer, asking God to help me somehow supernaturally forgive them.

Just after I did this, a whole sequence of thoughts occurred to me.

They happened one-by-one, but the whole experience ended up feeling like a ton of bricks. One after another, I had flashes of things I had done and thought in the past, flashes of my own sins, if you will. Regretful things, embarrassing things, things I cringed while remembering. These things came to my memory one after another—like a slideshow of my most terrible side.

Within those flashes and moments of conviction, I experienced a true awakening. I felt my anger and intolerance toward those who had wronged me slip away. I understood that I needed grace and forgiveness just as much as they did. Sure, it might be for other, less obvious reasons, but I needed it—I needed it something terrible. The memory collection of my failures made that crystal clear.

I blinked at the ceiling, realizing that tears had been streaming down the sides of my face, and now there were pools of tears on each side of my head.

"Oh my gosh," I whispered, wiping my face as I realized what had just happened.

I had said a lot of prayers in my life, and if I'm being honest, most of them were when I was in a pinch, or needed God's help. I had never, in all my prayers got an immediate answer, but this time I did. I asked God to help me forgive others, and He did so by letting me flash back to my own sins—a collection of shortcomings. At first, it was just the memories, but before long, I realized that these thoughts were causing me to feel differently toward others—to forgive them.

It was humbling and amazing, and I was in awe that my prayer had been answered on the spot like that, and that it was answered by the most unlikely means. I even flashed back to a few times when I had no idea I was doing something wrong, and my actions or words *still* hurt someone else.

I glanced at the clock by my bedside to find that I had been lost in thought for the past hour. I sat up and found that the spots of tears that stained my blue comforter were about the size of baseballs. I took a deep breath, literally feeling like a weight had been lifted from my chest—and all because I realized that I was just as guilty as all of my offenders. It was beautiful and liberating, and I giggled at the absurdity of it all as I wiped my cheeks.

I was still smiling from the whole experience when Collin got to my apartment a little while later.

"Have you been crying?" he asked as he came inside.

"A little, but it was good."

I took his coat from him and hung it in the nearby coat closet as he took off his shoes. I came to stand in front of him, smiling even though my eyes still stung a little bit.

"You sure you're okay?" he asked, thinking my puffy eyes might have something to do with me being sick.

"You were right," I said, popping up to place a thankful kiss on his cheek. "I think what you said about drinking rat poison got me thinking. I asked God for help with forgiveness, and I got it. It was crazy. I never had a prayer instantly answered before. Anyway, I feel better, and I'm sorry. I'm sorry you had to come way over here. I should have stuck around at the restaurant." I reached up and put my hand on his face, running my fingertips through the hair above his ear.

He gave me a slow blink along with a lazy smile, telling me he enjoyed my touch. "So you just all of a sudden feel better?" he asked.

"I think I might," I said skeptically. "I really don't understand it myself, but I definitely have a new attitude toward giving other people grace—even my dad." I smiled, feeling relieved that I was no longer mad at him.

"I told Elaina you were jealous," he said with a sly but still sleepy grin. "She got a kick out of that."

"No you did not," I said with the type of shocked expression that made him smile. "What'd you say?"

"She text me asking about applying for a job, and I told her she almost got me in trouble."

I shrugged. "I knew I could take her; I just didn't want to start a fight in your restaurant," I teased.

He smiled at me. "You think you could take her, huh?"

I nodded and put up my dukes in the most confident boxer pose I knew. I had practiced my dukes-up pose in the mirror lots of times in the past, and I could tell Collin appreciated it because his smile broadened. He took a deep breath, in through his nose, letting his chest rise as his back bowed, and then let it out again, going back to a relaxed stance.

"I should have really booked a weekend at home. I don't know what I was thinking."

He was so spent, he could hardly keep his eyes open, but he was still wearing a groggy half-smile.

I reached out and touched him on the shoulder. "Can I get you a glass of orange juice and a neck rub?"

He peered out of one eye. "Am I dead?" he asked.

"No, why?" I asked, giggling.

"Because, those two things would be heaven right now.

Chapter 12

I had no idea how multi-faceted forgiveness could be. Before I had that experience, I thought forgiveness was just a word that described my feelings toward the event that happened and the person or persons who caused said event.

But somewhere in the midst of those memories, my perspective shifted. I understood how much more there was to forgiveness. It was after I realized how needy of grace I was that I was able to truly have grace in my heart to forgive others. It was amazing to me that a revelation of my own flaws was what freed me from assuming the worst of others. I had no idea how it happened, but it did. Just like that, my burden was gone.

Collin was still at my house. He had been there for a little over an hour that night. I no longer saw him through the filter of doubt, so it was like I was meeting him for the first time. I couldn't stop smiling. We were sitting on the couch together, but facing the television, which was turned off. His arm was wrapped around me, and I had my head on his shoulder.

"I should get home," he said. I could tell by his voice that he was reluctant to leave but knew he had to.

"I know." I sat up, stretching before I turned to look at him with a lazy smile.

Collin stayed in the same position, staring at me patiently. "Come to London," he said. "Ireland, actually. I have a little down time when I'm there, and I'm going to Dublin for a few days. Why don't you meet me there?"

"Dublin?"

"Yeah. I don't know why I didn't think of it sooner." He paused and rubbed his eyebrows. "I think I totally forgot I was even doing that. That's how busy I've been."

"Send me your itinerary sometime when you're thinking about it," I said. "I'll see what your dates are, and if it'd even be possible to make something like that happen. And in the meantime, please let me know if there's anything I can do to help at any of your restaurants."

He grinned at me. "You better be careful, or I'll put you to work."

"I will work," I said. "I mean, I'd love to help out if you need anything. I'm right here."

"Right where?" he asked, pulling me into his arms. I got off balance, and fell into his lap with a squeal, looking up at him in this new and improved, closer proximity.

"Right where?" he asked again. This time, our faces were only a few inches apart, and I stared right into his eyes, which were a multi-faceted grey-green in the dim light of my living room.

"Right here," I said breathlessly.

"Unless you come wi me to Dublin," he said. Only, he said the words in a perfect Irish accent that had my eyes bulging.

"Can you say other stuff like that?" I asked, thinking an accent sounded incredibly attractive on him.

"Aye, otherwise how would I get along in Ireland?" he asked.

His accent was perfect. I giggled at how good it was.

"Are you Irish?" I asked.

"I'm jus the bloody class clown who's got to be the center of attention all the time."

His accent was so perfect that I assumed he must have spent an extended amount of time there.

"You're so great a that." I said sincerely as I stared at him with adoration.

He smiled and said, "You like that?" in his normal, American accent.

"I love it," I said. "Can you do others?"

He nodded confidently.

"What can you do?"

"Anything. Australian, Italian, Spanish."

"Do another one," I said.

He shook his head. "Nope."

"Why not?"

"Because then you'd see the comedy in it."

"What is it you think I'm seeing now?" I asked, scanning his face. It was only inches from mine.

"You tell me," he said in that same perfect Irish accent.

"What was the question?" I asked after a few seconds of thinking about that accent and getting lost staring at his mouth.

"I was telling you why I'm not gonna bust out my Nacho Libre imitation," he said, in his normal voice. "The Irish one's enough for now. I like how it makes you look at me. Plus, I want to leave you with that one so it can entice you to meet me in Dublin."

"And you can't show me all your cool tricks on the first night," I said.

He smirked at me in that confident way all cool guys knew how to do. "That's nothing," he said. "I could show you all my accents tonight, and I'd still just go on impressing you for years. I've got way more than just accents."

I knew enough about his personality to know that he was kidding around, but there was something to a man having confidence, even if it was in a tongue-in-cheek way.

"I can't wait for that," I said.

"For what?"

"To be impressed," I said. "I love being impressed."

Just then, we heard the sounds of Lu at the door. She fiddled with it for a second, before it opened, and she looked at us with an apologetic expression. "I'm so sorry," she said. "I tried to text."

"I was on my way out anyway," Collin said. He patted my thigh before getting to his feet, and I stood up as well since I was halfway on his lap and planning on walking him out, anyway.

"No, no, I didn't mean to make you leave," Lu said with her hands up as she tiptoed reluctantly into the room. She pointed to the hallway. "I'm headed for the shower."

"I was standing up to walk out, anyway," Collin said. "Sarah showed me some of your art. I think it would be a good fit for one of my restaurants. Are you willing to take commissions if I give you the subject matter and dimensions for a few pieces?"

"Definitely," Lu said with no hesitation whatsoever. "That'd be amazing."

"It'll be another month or so before I can talk to you about it or make any plans, but I just wanted to see if it was something you'd be interested in."

Lu beamed at him. "For sure. Definitely. I'm ready when you are."

Collin glanced at me with a smile that said he needed to go.

"I'm gonna walk him to the elevator," I said, talking to Lu, but not taking my eyes off of Collin.

"Okay," she said, absentmindedly as she walked away, trying to seem like she wasn't paying the slightest bit of attention to us. "Bye Collin," she called from over her shoulder.

"Bye Lu."

Collin texted his driver to tell him he was on his way downstairs. He slipped his coat and shoes on by the door. I helped him into his coat, which was big and heavy, and he shrugged into it, thanking me for the help.

"I'm glad you let me come over," he said as we started out into the hallway. "I was sad to leave without seeing you."

I smiled because all the things that crossed my mind as a response seemed too serious or committal. I thought about saying, "I love you," or "I was sad about you leaving, too," but I just couldn't get those words out of my mouth. I settled for a smile even though I wanted to do something crazy like proclaim my love. Then I realized it was my turn to speak and I hadn't responded to Collin's last statement, which was simple but still heartfelt.

"What?" I asked feeling speechless.

"Goodnight, Sarah," he said sweetly as he smiled and reached out to touch the down arrow on the elevator.

"Goodnight," I said. "I miss you already."

He gave me a slow smile, as he reached out to lightly touch my hand. "I'm right here," he said, barely hanging onto me. The elevator dinged and opened at that very moment, leaving us with no other choice but to smile at each other.

"Not for long," I whispered.

He reached out and put his hand in front of the door to hold it open.

"Come to Dublin."

I smiled. "Maybe," I said. "Either way, I'll see you soon." I reached out and put my hand on one of his cheeks before stretching up to kiss the other. I used the force of my hand to press his cheek into me, giving me the leverage for a nice, firm kiss.

"I'm glad you came over, too," I said. "Thank you for making time for it on a day like today."

He leaned down and placed a quick farewell kiss right on my lips. "Thanks for the neck rub," he said with a smile and nod as he reluctantly broke away from me to get into the elevator.

"Bye Collin," I said.

"Bye Sarah."

He pressed the button to go to the first floor, and stood back, smiling at me as the doors closed. He picked up his hand to wave at me, and the sight of it was so glorious that I turned my shoulders and hips to the side and jumped sideways through the ever-narrowing crack in the elevator doors.

I literally barely made it through.

One second, the doors were closing, and the next I was jumping through them in a daring feat of acrobatics. I had to hoist myself so fervently into the elevator in order to avoid the closing doors that I landed right in Collin's arms. He caught me, laughing at the fact that I made him step backward with the impact.

"I'll ride down with you," I said, stating the obvious since the elevator was already moving by the time we gained our balance.

"I knew you were gonna do that," he said, his chest shaking with laughter as he held me tight.

"You did?" I asked. "How? *I* didn't even know I was gonna do it."

"I could see that faraway look in your eye right before you jumped," he said, still chuckling at me.

I pulled back to stare at him, and he shifted so that he could peer down at me. I thought he would say something, but he didn't, he just leaned down and kissed me. I opened my mouth this time, and he let his tongue touched my bottom lip before he drew it into his mouth. It was so warm and comfortable that I wished I could stay there forever. I barely had time to think before the elevator dinged and came to a stop. I hated it for moving so quickly.

"Come to Dublin, my love," he whispered in the Irish accent.

"I smiled and popped up to kiss his cheek as he reluctantly switched places with me so he could get out of the elevator.

"You're not playing fair," I said. "That accent's making me *have* to go."

"That's the whole idea," he said with a smile and wink as he stepped out of the elevator. I watched him as far as I could see without sticking my head out of the elevator.

"Hold the door," I heard a girl's voice say before it closed completely. I reached out and stopped it so that she could get on.

The first thing she did was stare at the numbers, and it wasn't until she looked at me with a confused expression that I noticed I hadn't pressed the button for my floor. The door closed as she pressed 8, and then I reached out to press 12, for myself.

"That was the dude from Best Chef," she said.

She spoke loudly and had a slightly aggressive tone to her voice that had me disinterested in continuing a conversation with her. I just smiled a little when she glanced at me, assuming her statement didn't necessarily require a response.

I caught myself wanting to write her off and not engage simply because of her tone, and then it hit me that I undoubtedly used the wrong tone sometimes by accident or out of nerves. I felt the urge to give her the benefit of the doubt instead of assuming the worst.

"Collin," I said. "He is on Best Chef."

"He your boyfriend or something?" she asked, leaning back to stare at me.

I shrugged. "I think. I wish. Probably," I said.

Her expression, the one that had been a complete scowl, softened a little as she looked at me. "You're pretty," she said, surprising me.

"Thank you," I said. "You are too."

She smiled shyly and looked down. "Well, I think you can get him if you ask me," she said as the elevator door opened to her floor and she stepped off.

"Thank you!" I called as she walked away.

The door closed and I rode up to my floor with a huge grin on my face, feeling thankful for the way that encounter had played out and amazed that the concept of forgiveness could be applied to everyday situations like that.

Chapter 13

"Oh, my gosh, I'm so sorry I interrupted you," was the first thing Lu said when I came back into my apartment.

"You didn't," I said. "He really did have to go."

She had poured herself a bowl of cereal, and she carried it into the living room so she could come talk to me.

"He's soooo cute," she moaned around a mouth full of food.

"He's so sweet," I said. "I feel like he's my brother or something—instant comfort, you know? Have you ever had that?"

She made a face like she was trying to remember before switching her expression to a silly one. "Noooo," she said. "Of course not, or I wouldn't be so painfully single."

"Single's not so painful," I said.

"It's having *that* attitude that gets you un-single," she said.

"Probably. I definitely wasn't looking for Collin."

"It's the same with jobs," she said. "They're easier to find when you don't need one."

"How was work?" I asked.

"Same. Good. We had music tonight."

"Did you make some good tips?"

"Okay," she said, chewing and smiling. "Drake came by. He's still seeing that Beckett girl."

"Was she with him?" I asked.

Lu nodded. "She had a few of her friends with her. They knew the guy who was singing. Drake took some pictures of him." Lu scrolled through her phone and flashed the screen at me. "He got this one of me working the espresso machine," she said.

"That's a great picture," I said, meaning it. It was beautiful. "I love your profile."

"Aww, thanks," she said taking another look at it. "He said he got some others of me, but he hasn't been able to go through them yet."

"You should make him get some pictures of you drawing," I said. "You could use them for your social media. I loved the ones he did for me."

"I can't believe Collin wants to buy some of my art," she said. "I've never had a commission before. I'm nervous. What if he doesn't like what I come up with?"

"He sees your style," I said gesturing at the countless works in progress she had in her little corner of the room. "You have a certain style, and he liked it, otherwise he wouldn't have asked you."

"I can't believe you're dating Collin Ross," she said, shaking her head. "That's so weird."

"Why's that so weird? I'm around famous people all the time, remember?"

"Yeah, but he's different. He's... he's like a man," she said.

I laughed. "What's that supposed to mean?"

"I don't know. He's different. He's so *business* oriented. He's got all these plans and stuff going on."

"I knowww," I whispered, dazedly as I thought about watching Collin interact with the staff and customers at his restaurant. "He wants me to go to Dublin."

"Ireland?"

"No. Dublin, Ohio." I was in an out-of-sorts mood, so I easily held a straight face when I said it.

"Are you messing with me?" she asked.

"About the Ohio thing, yes, but not about him asking me to go with him to Dublin."

"He wants you to go to Ireland?" she asked.

I nodded.

"When?"

I shrugged. "Coming up. I don't have the exact dates, but this month sometime."

"Are you going?"

I shrugged. "He just asked me like five minutes ago. I haven't even thought about it."

"What's there to think about?" she asked. "I've heard you say you wanted to go to Ireland before."

"I know."

"So go."

"I probably will," I said, feeling a sense of excitement starting to build.

"Is he Irish?" she asked.

"Who, Collin? No, I don't think so. I don't know, though. He can do an amazing Irish accent."

"The name Collin is Irish, I think. Did you say he had an Irish accent?"

"Just when he wants to," I said.

She smiled longingly as she set the empty cereal bowl on the coffee table. "Did he really do an accent for you? That's so cute."

"It was more hot than cute," I said, lifting the front of my shirt up and down to cool myself off.

Lu giggled. "You are so adorable right now," she said.

I smiled and shook my head, knowing I was blushing.

"You have to go to Ireland," she said. "What if he asks you to marry him?"

"When?" I asked, thinking she meant when we were in Ireland, which embarrassingly enough, had already crossed my mind.

Lu shrugged. "Whenever," she said. "Like eventually. What if you two wind up getting married? I could say I was there when you met. I remember that day when he called you sunshine."

"Yep. I remember. And I bet we will get married. Isn't that crazy?"

"I can't believe you're acting like this, Sarah." She lifted her hands in surrender as if apologizing in advance for what she was about to say. "I mean I really thought I would have to move back in here after I finish my time at S&S just to keep you from dying alone."

We both laughed. "Thanks a lot," I said.

"No really, I'm so glad to see you like this."

I shrugged. "I was scared," I said. "Even as recently as tonight I was scared. I took a cab home behind his back and was planning on not seeing him again. Then, all of a sudden, (a pause to snap my fingers) I just got un-scared. I know it seems crazy, but I prayed right before it happened, and I really think the two were related."

"What are you saying? You did a 180 just like that and went back to not having trust issues?"

"Yes," I said with a little laugh. "I can't quite explain it, but I did."

I didn't bother telling Lu that it was deeper than that. I didn't tell her about the sequence of memories that led to my shift in perspective. One, because it was a bunch of shameful stuff, and two because I thought I wasn't usually one for getting deep and discussing my feelings.

"How'd he like his necklace?" she asked after taking a few seconds to think about everything I had said.

"He loved it," I said. "He told me thank you about ten times. I caught him touching it and turning it over in his fingers."

"I saw he was wearing it," she said. "It looked good." She smiled, and her eyes got wide. "You think he's gonna wear it on the show?" she asked.

I laughed at how giddy and impressed she was by the idea. "Probably," I said.

"Speaking of show," she said, pushing at my leg. "Macy heard a rumor that Theo Duval was talking to Netflix about doing a documentary on Shower & Shelter."

"Seriously? Is it true?"

Lu shrugged. "She said she heard it from Lane, and his word is pretty dependable. But Macy said not to say anything. They haven't made any official announcements or anything."

"What if they decide to do it when you're living there?" I asked.

"I'm sure if they do it, it *will* be when I'm living there. I move in this August, and I can stay for up to two years as long as I don't get kicked out."

"As if you would ever get kicked out," I said.

"People have," she said. "They do. Their rules are pretty strict. They have to be that way to keep everything in order. Thirty artist in tight quarters on the same floor of an apartment building could easily get chaotic."

"What do you mean strict?"

"No overnight guests—not even boyfriends or girlfriends. Artists only sleep in the loft. Mr. Duval said he wanted to provide what he felt like he needed as a struggling artist and nothing more—a shower and a shelter. He's not trying to give us a place to stay so we can just sit around and party. Lane made a point of saying that."

"I still don't quite understand why he does it," I said. "But I guess there's really no reason for me to even try. Maybe he really does just want to help people out, and there are no strings attached."

"I keep telling you that, and you don't get it."

"I might now. Or at least I'm willing to have a little faith that it might be the case."

She reached out and pinched me with a teasing grin. "You are soooo bit by the love bug right now."

"Whaaat?" I asked in a high-pitched voice.

"You are. He did an accent for you. That's adorable. You have to go to Dublin."

"Aye," I said. "I think I just might." I tried my best to make it sound like an Irish accent, but it came out a little too growl-y."

"Arrrr, you sound like a pirate," Lu said, contorting her face in her best imitation of Captain Blackbeard.

I cracked up, knowing she was right. "Arr, matey," I said with my hand in a hook position. "I must be sailin' the high seas for Ireland where I'll get my booty!"

I totally meant it in a *pirate booty* way, but Lu and I both cracked up like a couple of little schoolgirls when the phrase came out of my mouth.

"Oh my gosh, you can *never, ever* try an Irish accent on him," she said, regaining her composure after laughing. "You seriously turned into a pirate."

My phone rang, and I put it to my ear, mouthing the name 'Collin' to Lu.

"Hey," I said, once I knew the call connected.

"Hey, I just found out I'll be in Dublin on the twentieth for three nights. Then I go back to London for a week, and then I'm home."

"That's right after your birthday," I said.

"I know. It's a good thing you already gave my present."

"Yep, and it looks good on you."

"Yes it does!" Lu called, leaning over to speak into the phone. She knew I was talking about his necklace, and I was fine with her yelling at him. She and I smiled at each other.

"I tried to do an Irish accent for Lu, and it came out sounding like a pirate."

Lu slapped a hand to her forehead at the fact that I was confessing.

"Irish is close to pirate," Collin said in a serious tone, like he was familiar with my hardships. "They're in the same family, for sure."

I was trying to think of something dry and witty, but I couldn't hold back a giggle.

"Does that mean you're coming?"

"Does what mean I'm coming?"

"You were trying to do the accent for Lu."

"Oh," I said. "I think so."

"You're coming?"

"Yeah."

"Good. I'll set up your hotel and flight. Just let me know when you're ready to book it, and I'll have someone take care of it for you."

"I'm ready," I said, without even thinking about it. My heart started pounding the second I said it, and I made a wide-eyed expression at Lu, who returned it, but otherwise did her best not to seem too curious.

"I'll get your reservations," Collin said.

"I don't mind paying for it," I said.

"You're my guest," he said. "I invited you."

"I've always wanted to go there."

Lu pressed her knee into my thigh even though we weren't looking at each other.

"It's the twentieth, okay?" Collin asked.

"Yep."

"You sure that's okay?" he persisted as if he could tell I was slightly out-of-it and hadn't actually looked at a calendar.

"It's fine," I said, since I would literally move *anything* on my calendar to go to Ireland and be with him.

"I'm so glad you're coming," he said. "I have three days completely off. I'm not doing anything with a restaurant while I'm in Dublin, other than eating at them."

"I can't wait."

"Good. I'll call you tomorrow."

"Okay," I said.

I told Collin goodbye and disconnected the call, turning to look at Lu in the process.

"Is he buying your ticket?" she asked.

I nodded.

"I tried to hear what he was saying, but I couldn't. I was just glad he didn't ask you to try out your pirate impression," she added, being silly.

I laughed and sank my face into my hands at the thought. "I would never!" I said. "He was seriously hot when he did his. I just sounded like a big dork."

"It really wasn't all that bad," Lu said. "If your dad ever makes a TV show about pirates, you could try out for it."

"What's the weather in Ireland in March?" I asked since my thoughts were going in about a thousand different directions.

"Google it," she said with a shrug.

We both stared at our respective devices for a few seconds. "Looks like it's warmer there than it is here," she said. She glanced at me, and we both made wacky faces at each other.

"I can't believe I'm doing this," I said.

She shook her head at me. "I can. I'm so happy to see you happy. What if you get to see Stonehenge?"

"I'm sure we're staying in Ireland," I said. "He said we'd only be there a few days."

"I thought that's where Stonehenge was," she said.

"I think it's in England."

"Really? I always thought it was in Ireland. Are you sure you're thinking of what I'm thinking of?"

I tilted my head at her. "The big rocks, standing on end in a circle?" I asked.

She nodded.

"That's in England."

Her expression was genuinely confused as she shrugged. "Really?"

I nodded.

"You sure? England? The big rocks?"

I nodded again.

"Well, it should be in Ireland," she said.

Chapter 14

Collin wouldn't arrive in Dublin until the afternoon of the twentieth, but my flight got there pretty early that morning. It was a non-stop, overnight flight, so I managed to get a few hours sleep while we flew.

I was scheduled to arrive at 9am, and knowing that Collin wouldn't get there until later that evening, I planned to check into my hotel room and try to get a little more rest. I wanted to see Dublin and everything, but more than that, I wanted to see Collin, and I didn't want to be completely exhausted.

We had talked every day in the weeks since he had been London, and I was letting him into my heart in a way that I thought was lost to me. He was in my thoughts and plans, and I was absolutely overjoyed that I was about to see him.

I had done some traveling in my life, but I had never flown into an airport where the land below was as lush and green as it was in Ireland. From the moment the plane started its decent, I had the feeling I had gone back in time.

A driver was waiting for me at the airport, and he brought me to the hotel, a place called The Merrion, which was in the center of the city. I was taken aback by how small Dublin was. I always thought of it as a booming metropolis like New York, and it was far smaller than I anticipated.

There was a lot of stone in New York, but nothing like Dublin, and that might have been what had me feeling like I had stepped into a time machine. The hotel had an undeniable old-world quality about it, too, with drawing rooms, fireplaces, and brocade fabrics.

My room was immaculate, and I felt comfortable the instant I stepped into it. It was a one bedroom suite in the main house, beautifully appointed with light furniture and bedding. It was crisp and clean, and I felt like I was the Queen of Ireland.

I flopped onto the bed, where I stayed for the next two hours. I was too excited to sleep, but I made myself try for two whole hours before I decided my attempts were futile.

I freshened up before heading out for a late lunch. There were a thousand pubs in Dublin, so I had a plethora of choices within walking distance of the hotel. Most of the time, I would check reviews and make plans, but this time I felt like setting out and seeing where my feet took me.

My plans to have anti-plans worked out when someone on the street saw that I was a tourist, pointed at a random pub, and told me I should have lunch there. I heeded their advice, and went into the pub, taking a seat at one of the few open stools at the bar. I took a picture of myself with the pub sign in the background and sent it to Collin along with a text that read, "I think I'm in Dublin."

I knew his flight wouldn't arrive until later that evening, and before then, he had a lot going on, so I didn't expect to hear from him... I just wanted him to know I was excited to be there.

The barkeeper was funny and entertaining, and I didn't feel the slightest bit awkward about being there alone. He recommended something authentically Irish for me to eat, and helped me make conversation with the people sitting next to me. They were all so nice, telling me things I should do and see while I was in Ireland.

I sat there for the next few hours, talking and laughing with the barkeeper and the people coming in and out of the pub.

Collin had made a point of telling me that, to him, Dublin was all about the characters who lived there, so I made an effort to take as much of it in as I could. I talked to a few people from other places in Europe, and one other American, but by in large, they were locals, which was so much fun for me. I loved an Irish accent and giggled every time I had to ask them to repeat something.

On my right, was a man named John. He and his wife, Ellen, had been sitting next to me for about the last hour. They were the sweetest couple ever, and we had a fine time joking around and getting to know one another. We were all laughing at something Luke, the bartender, had said when a stranger came in and sat on the stool at my left.

I was enjoying my conversation with John and Ellen, so I virtually had my back turned towards the person who sat down. I saw John and Ellen acknowledge him, so in friendly, Dublin-like fashion, I turned to do the same.

"Do ya mind?" the man asked me, nodding as if to indicate that he was wondering if his stool was already taken.

"It's open," Luke said, sliding a menu in front of the man.

Collin.

It was Collin.

Collin Ross.

My Collin was sitting in the barstool next to me, smiling at me casually like it was the first time we had ever met.

"Her neme's Sarah," John said, leaning over to speak to Collin.

It was apparent by the fluctuation he used in his tone that he was proud to introduce me—like he thought Collin might be impressed. Ellen elbowed him for this.

"Sarah," Collin said, nodding at me like it was the first time he was making my acquaintance.

His pretending not to know me wasn't even the most hilarious thing. The wildest part was that he was speaking with an Irish accent in front of all these *real* Irish people. I just stared at him, wondering how in the world he was so calm and collected when doing something so out-of-his-mind.

His dark hair and light eyes made him look completely at home here. After being in Dublin all day, my conclusion was that Collin could easily pass as a handsome Irishman.

"Collin," he said with a nod.

"Cheers, Collin," John said. "Sarah here was just telling us she knows the people who bought the Banks estate," John continued with great pride. He had a Guinness with his lunch, and he had gotten chattier and chattier as the hour passed.

"Aye, the Banks' place, eh?" Collin asked, acting like he knew what the guy was talking about.

"Her da's a big Hollywood movie-maker." Ellen explained proudly.

I looked at Collin, who was pretending to give me an appraising stare. I wanted to throw myself at him, but I held back. "So, you've got friends in Dublin?" Collin asked, since this was the first he had heard about me knowing someone there.

"I found out my dad has an old friend who lives here," I explained in a voice that cracked with nerves. "I wasn't planning on seeing them on my trip, though."

"She's here to meet her boyfriend," Ellen announced, a little more loudly than she intended.

"Your boyfriend, eh?" Collin said, pulling back to stare at me with an appraising grin.

"Aye, and ya better not get any big ideas," Ellen said, "because he's some big-time Hollywood actor, too."

"I'm not scared of a Hollywood actor," Collin said contemptuously, continuing to use that perfect (thank goodness) Irish accent.

I was terrified for him that he would break character and get caught, but he was completely, one hundred percent in character, and no one seemed to know the difference.

My heart raced at the silly deception of it all, and I had to work to contain the giddy grin that constantly wanted to break across my face. He was far and away the most handsome guy in the pub, the most handsome guy I'd ever seen, and I just sat there and blinked at him, feeling dazed and all shaken-up.

"He's not a Hollywood actor," Luke said, slipping a napkin and a glass of water in front of Collin. "He's a pub owner."

"Restaurants," John said.

"I could take some fancy pub owner any dey," Collin said. He slapped his hand over his fist, indicating that he'd like to hit someone.

"Ye two need to leave the girl alone," Ellen said. "She's all excited to see her man."

"He's probably American," Collin said, rolling his eyes and causing everyone sitting around to laugh.

"He is American," Ellen said protectively. "And ye two better mind yer own business, because she's in love. She said she's gonna marry him." Ellen smiled at me and nodded as if it was the least she could do to make that little announcement on my behalf.

I just stared at her with my heart pounding, trying to remember what I had said and how much trouble she was about to get me into.

"She's gonna marry him, eh?" Collin asked with wide eyes.

My heart continued to pound in those seconds when everyone was waiting for my response. Every second felt like an eternity. "He *is* an American," I said, trying to maintain my composure in the midst of all the nerves and chaos happening in my thoughts.

"Yes, but do ya love him?" Collin asked, hanging his coat on the back of his barstool.

"I do," I said, heart pounding, "even though it's none of your business."

My voice was trembling for two reasons: one because I would never in real life tell a stranger it was none of their business, and two because it *was* his business. It was very much his business.

"Then why isn't the fool here wi ya right now?" he asked, still staring at me as he continued the Irish charade.

"Because he has to work," I said.

He scoffed. "If ye were mine, I would never leave ya in this pub to talk to the likes of me and this bunch."

"Oh, yeah?" I asked. "What would you do?"

"I'd drag ya off and marry ya," he said.

My heart raced even faster as a result of him saying those words. What's more was that he stared at me as if he was completely serious. I wanted to throw myself into his arms, shout *yes, yes, yes,* and call that our official proposal. It was with great difficulty that I refrained from doing so.

Collin and I sat there for nearly an hour, talking to the people at the pub while he ate. We mostly kept at the act, although there was nothing I could do to stop myself from flirting with him a little bit since he was so irresistible.

Just before I left, Ellen asked if I would go with her to the restroom. I agreed, and she followed me in there, making an intense expression as if she wanted to talk about some matters that were life or death.

"Well, ye've got to *consider him*, at least," she said in a pleading tone.

I cocked my head to the side, having no idea what she was talking about. "Collin!" she whispered, gesturing into the pub. "I know yer here to meet yer boyfriend and everythin, but Sarah dear, sometimes ye have to trow caution to da wind, sweetheart. Sometimes, you have to recognize a connection when ye have one."

I had to work hard to contain a nervous giggle at the sight of her intense expression. She had been watching me interact with Collin, and really thought we had a chance. It was the sweetest thing ever, and even though I wanted to tell her the truth, I wouldn't for Collin's sake since I didn't want him to get caught using a fake accent.

"You mean me and him?" I asked, pointing toward the bar.

"Yes!" she insisted in a whisper. "He's such a nice young man, and he likes ya. Don't tell me ya don't see it."

"He did offer to walk me back to my hotel," I said.

She smiled and nodded like she thought that would be a great idea. "Ya should do it," she said. "Give him a chance lass. Ya only live once."

"Yo-lo," I said with a little grin.

Ellen furrowed her eyebrows and cocked her head at me curiously, which made me smile.

"Yo-lo," I repeated. "You-only-live-once."

"Ah, yes!" she said triumphantly when she understood. "Yo-lo, Sarah, yo-lo, dear."

Chapter 15

Ellen and I came out of the ladies room together and found our place at the bar, which had grown more and more crowded as the afternoon passed.

"I need to get back to my hotel," I said as soon as we arrived at our seats. I still had to settle my tab, so I sat on the edge of my barstool.

"I guess I'll walk ya," Collin said, motioning for Luke to bring the check. "I'll take mine, too," he called to the barkeeper.

I started to dig in my purse, but Collin put his hand out to stop me. I glanced at him, and he gave me a narrow-eyed smile that broke character a little bit, telling me I was crazy if I thought I was paying. I smiled back at him as Luke slid our tickets onto the bar.

"I'll get the lady's," Collin said sliding the tickets and his credit card back toward Luke.

"Yo-lo," Ellen said, although it was disguised in a cough.

This struck me as so funny and cute that I widened my eyes at Collin and gave him a pleading expression, saying I had to get out of there before I blew our cover. Knowing we had to wait on Luke to bring the ticket, he answered with an easy, patient smile that had my insides feeling warm and melty.

"Yep, Sarah was sayin' she might need help gettin' back to her hotel," Ellen said.

"Ellen," John said, scolding his wife for overstepping her bounds.

She made an injured expression. "Wha? She already said she wouldn't mind the company."

"I wouldn't," I said with a shy shrug.

"See?" Ellen said. "She said she wouldn't mind."

"Are we off, then?" Collin asked, with a nod at me as he stood.

"Sure," I said. We said goodbye to John, Ellen, Luke, and the others sitting around us at the bar, and headed for the door. Collin opened the door, and I walked past him. I was so anxious to see him that it was almost impossible to refrain from latching onto him.

"Wait for it..." he said through clinched teeth as I walked past him with a hungry expression on my face.

I made sure we were past the pub windows when I finally let myself grab him.

"Oh, my gosh, I can't believe we did that just now," I said. "I can't believe that just happened. I'm so nervous, it feels like I robbed a bank or something."

I brought his hand to my heart as we continued to walk down the sidewalk. He reached out, wrapping his other arm around me and pulling me into a giant bear hug, and I glanced behind me to make sure John and Ellen weren't spying on us.

"Why's that make you so nervous?" he asked, laughing at me like he thought my anxiousness was cute.

"Because. What if they would have caught you talking like that? Weren't *you* nervous?"

"Not as nervous as ye were," he said, lapsing back into the accent for a second.

"How are you so confident?" I said, feeling genuinely amazed. "I would *never* have the guts to do that."

He shrugged. "I mean, if some American came into my restaurant speaking with a slightly-off American accent, I wouldn't say anything," he said reasonably. "I wouldn't think anything of it. Would you?"

I thought about what he was saying, and knew he was probably right. "You sounded just like them," I said. "I guess I was just afraid you'd get caught."

He laughed, squeezing me. "Even if I *did* get caught, none of them would care. They'd probably get a kick out of it."

I sighed again. "That was seriously the funniest thing I've ever done," I said, still feeling out-of-it with adrenaline as we began to walk. I glanced over my shoulder again. "I feel kinda bad, though. Ellen drug me to the bathroom saying I had to give you a chance. She was so sweet. She told me I only live once."

Collin slowed down and glanced behind us. "Did she really?" he asked.

I nodded.

"What'd she say?"

"She said she liked you and thought I should give you a chance."

"That's so nice," he said, sincerely.

"I know."

"You wanna go back and tell them the truth?" he asked, coming to a stop again.

People on the sidewalk (or footpath as they call it over there) stepped around us as we stood, deciding what to do.

"Really?" I asked.

He nodded. "I don't want you to feel bad about lying to them," he said. "I was just messing around. I don't care if they know."

"Really?" I asked again. I hadn't thought of it as lying, but now that he mentioned it, maybe I would feel better if we went back to tell them—not so much because I felt bad about lying to them, since I really didn't think of it that way. It was more about me being proud of Collin and wanting them to know he was my man. I liked the people I met at the pub, and I wanted them to know Collin and I went together.

"Are you sure?" I asked, leveling him with a sincere stare.

He shrugged easily. "If you want them to know, we'll tell them. I'm not worried about it." He smiled as he tugged me in the direction of the pub so that we could go back.

"I'm nervous," I said.

"Don't be," he said. "I'll handle it."

"What do you mean, you'll handle it?"

"I mean there's nothing for you to worry about because I have it under control."

"You do? What are you gonna do? Collin, what are we doing?" I whispered as he opened the door to the pub and he pulled me inside.

"Shhh," he said. He pulled me through the pub to the corner of the bar were Ellen and John were still sitting.

He held my hand and looked in control the entire time we walked. Our little corner of the room looked at us with great curiosity when they caught sight of us holding hands.

"It seems I'm actually the American she was waiting on," Collin said in his regular accent, smiling and making eye contact with them in that winning way he had.

"You're kiddin' me!" John said.

"I knew it!" Luke said, slapping his hand on the bar. "I told ye he was fekin' the accent."

"*I* didn't know it," Ellen said with an utterly stunned look on her face. "I had no idea. Were ye the American the whole time?"

Collin tried to hide his amusement at her question as he nodded at her, and she just continued to shake her head at him like she was completely bewildered.

"Were ye the American she's waitin' on, then?"

Collin nodded.

"Are ye both really called Collin?" she asked, still not fully getting it.

Collin smiled and put a hand on her shoulder. "I'm really only one Collin. I'm the American she was waiting on. I was him the whole time. We were pretending not to know each other."

Ellen smiled when understanding finally sank in, and then she shoved at Collin's shoulder playfully, knocking him back and causing us all to laugh.

"I told her to cheat on ye with ye!" she said.

"He thought that was sweet," I said, giggling.

"Now I'm not so sure," Collin said with a confused face that had everyone cracking up again.

"I knew it," Luke said. "He winked at me the second he sat down, and I knew somethin' was goin' on."

"Did ye know he was her American?" Ellen asked.

"Nay," Luke said. "But I knew he was playin' somehow."

"Well, I, for one am amazed," Ellen said.

"Me too," John said. He motioned to his own mouth. "I just thought ye had a little speech problem."

We were all laughing at that when Ellen said, "I knew ye two were meant to be somethin'. I knew it from the time ye sat down. Sarah's smile was lovely from the start, but it changed when this one came in." Again, she poked at Collin, who smiled at her.

"She's bonnie," Ellen added. "Not just her face, but on the inside, too."

"Aye," John agreed. "She's bonnie, indeed." He turned on his stool, trying to get a better look at Collin now that he knew who he was. "I think I know you now, come to think of it, from the cooking show."

"What cooking show?" Ellen asked.

"The one where they get voted off every week."

Ellen shrugged indicating she had no idea what her husband was talking about. "He loves to cook," she said. "He watches those cooking shows all the time, tryin' to learn tips and tricks. I don't like to cook, myself, but I don't mind cleaning up." She paused and stared at Collin for a few seconds before looking at us as a couple. "I just can't believe it," she said. "I feel like I should ask ye both for yer autograph or somethin'."

"I'd like to cover their tab," Collin said, handing Luke a few bills before we stepped to the side to let someone else sit at our old place at the bar.

Luke nodded graciously as he took the money. John and Ellen protested at first, but ultimately, they conceded to let Collin buy their lunch and thanked him profusely for doing so. I felt proud of the way Collin spoke to people and won them over. He was right; they didn't care at all that he'd been using a fake accent—if anything, they were impressed by it. People were always all-smiles when they looked at him, which made being the one on his arm that much more enjoyable.

Collin and I spent the next two hours walking around and going into shops before deciding to head back to our hotel. The sun had already set, and we were both tired, so we agreed to get some dinner in the room.

"That was the best day ever," I said as we walked down the hallway that led to our rooms. His was next to mine, and we came to it first.

"I told you Ireland's all about the characters."

"It's so cool," I said. "I can't believe how friendly everyone is."

"They're nice to you because you're the most beautiful thing they've ever seen," Collin said, coming to a stop in front of his door. He took me into his arms, and I went willingly, resting my arm on his chest and letting my hand absentmindedly toy with the button on his jacket collar.

"I am not," I said, feeling shy about his statement.

"Yes you are," he said, staring at me. "And I've seen a lot of beautiful things, so I know. You're the best one."

I giggled and reached up to touch his face, but I didn't even get to make contact because he turned to open his door.

"Let's order some dinner," he said, pulling me inside. His room was just like mine, and I went through the living room and into the bedroom where

I flopped onto the bed just like I did the instant I entered every hotel room.

Collin took off his jacket and kicked off his shoes before running into the bedroom to pounce onto the bed beside me. I bounced and then landed in a fit of giggles as I reached out to grab his face while he hovered over me. His face felt big in my grasp, and I loved the warmth of it under my fingertips.

"You're scruffy," I said, touching his short beard, which I loved. He leaned toward me, and gently rubbed his cheek on mine.

"I missed you," I said.

"Marry me," he whispered.

"Are you suddenly inspired?" I asked, knowing we were on a bed. I tried to control the rise and fall of my chest so that it wouldn't be obvious that I was nervous.

"I really just want to marry you," he said. "Not that I'm *uninspired*, because, really, you're an inspiring woman, Sarah. But it's not that. I'd marry you tomorrow and still wait a year if you asked me to."

"You would?" I asked.

He nodded.

"If I married you tomorrow, I wouldn't *want* to wait a year," I said, breathlessly.

"I know," he said.

"Well, if you know that, then it's not really a gesture, is it?"

He smiled. "Marry me, Sarah. I mean it. I love you."

I stared at him, searching the depths of his eyes in an effort to see if he was serious.

"I love you, too," I said.

We had said it on the phone, but never in person, and there was some sort of magic about looking at him when I said the words. I ran my fingertips along his eyebrow and then down the side of his eye, circling onto his cheekbone.

"Yes," I whispered with a completely serious look on my face. "I wish there were a word that meant something more than yes—some kind of resounding yes."

"You could just say, 'it's a resounding yes'," he said, being serious.

"Yeah, but I wish there was *one word* that meant the same thing."

"How about *heck yeah*?"

I shrugged. "Not really my style. And that's still two words."

"How about you just kiss me?" he asked. "That's a resounding yes without saying a word at all."

"Then…" I stretched up to place a quick but fervent kiss right on his lips like I had sealed some kind of deal.

He smiled. "Good," he said. "I have one more week in London when I leave here."

I nodded, since I was already familiar with his plans.

"I was planning on going home after that, maybe it would be fun to get married in Ireland. We should do it here."

"You mean when you're done in London?" I asked, pulling back a little to gauge how serious he was.

He nodded.

"In a week?"

He nodded again. "Let's call our families and fly them out here," he said with a shrug. "It's only six hours from New York. They'll drop what they're doing and fly over for a day or two."

"Are you for real?" I asked, sitting up on my shoulder and leaning over him.

"Think about it," he said. "I don't see any reason to wait."

"I really love you," I said, staring into his eyes.

He smiled. "I know," he said. "Otherwise, we wouldn't be having this conversation."

"I'm gonna marry you," I said.

He gave me an almost imperceptible nod. "In about ten days," he said, causing my stomach to tie into a thousand knots.

"Are you serious?" I asked.

"If you want to."

"I do," I whispered.

"Okay."

"Okay, so we're doing it?" I asked.

"Not till we're married," he said, pretending to misunderstand me.

"I thought you said we were gonna wait a year even after that," I said, teasing him.

"I did. I would. I could do a year standing on my head."

"I'm gonna marry you, Collin. Soon. And we're not waiting for anything after that."

"Uh-huh," he moaned, pulling me in and nestling his head comfortably into the crook of my neck.

"This is the best day ever," I whispered.

Chapter 16

It was almost midnight by the time I forced myself to get off the couch in Collin's room and head to my own. It was only 7pm in New York, so I shouldn't have been tired, but I hadn't had much sleep the night before, so my eyes were getting heavy. I was so tired that I forgot for a second that somewhere in the last few hours, Collin and I had agreed to get married. My stomach clinched just thinking about it.

Here I was, about to leave his room and go to mine, and somehow feeling incomplete or unsettled about it. We had discussed all sorts of wedding options, but neither of us had told our families, and that, combined with my exhaustion, sort of gave me the feeling that I had made everything up.

"I'll call my dad and see if we could do it at his friend's house," I said, when Collin walked me to the door. We had talked about trying to have our little impromptu wedding there, but mostly I was just bringing it up to make sure Collin was prepared for me to call my family and let them in on what we decided.

"You should call him," he said, pinching my side. "He'll need to start making plans. It's coming up."

The question that was on the forefront of my mind was, *what if they won't come?* But I didn't ask that. I just smiled at him like I was confident my parents would support this decision, which I was not. I was terrified to tell them what we had just decided, but the idea of *not* marrying Collin was absolutely more terrifying than dealing with their reaction.

"What?" he whispered, noticing that I was in deep thought.

I grinned. "Nothin'."

He reached out and gave a little tug to the front of my shirt, pulling me toward him. "Come back right when you wake up," he said.

"First thing," I promised, kissing his cheek.

He pulled me into his arms using a hand around my back. "Night."

"Night," I said.

And just like that, he let go, and I turned and walked away. I went into my room feeling numb and discombobulated. I hadn't been in there since before I left for lunch that day, and so much happened since then that it felt like it had been three days. I hadn't quite had my daily regimen of caffeine, and to top it off, I needed a shower. I was exhausted and somewhat overwhelmed as I meandered into my quiet room. I turned on the television so that I wouldn't feel so alone. I took a shower and climbed into bed, hoping and assuming that I would fall asleep as soon as my head hit the pillow.

It didn't happen that way.

I lay there till 2am, feeling unable to turn off my brain. It was only 9 o'clock in New York, so I decided to call my parents, hoping that telling them my big news would help me sleep.

"Is everything okay?" were the first words out of my mom's mouth.

"Fine," I said. "Dublin's awesome. It's so beautiful over here. So many stones."

"I saw that picture you posted on your Facebook," she said. "Looks like that gentleman made it over there."

"Collin," I said.

"Uh-huh."

"That's why I'm calling," I said.

"Why?"

"Because I'm deciding, I decided to marry him. We're gonna get married. We're getting married."

My mom stayed silent for a few seconds.

"Soon," I added.

She let out a sharp laugh like she thought I was clearly joking.

"Really, mom. That's why I'm calling you. I was gonna see if Dad could talk to those friends of his, the Steiners, to see if we could maybe do the wedding at their place. Something small. I met some people today who showed me pictures of it, and it's amazing."

"Sarah Lynn!" My mom's voice pierced into my ear in a sharp and shrill tone.

"What, mom?" I asked, feeling injured at how frantic she sounded.

"I do *not* appreciate you calling me like this, young lady. It's hard enough that you're all the way over there on the other side of the earth. The last thing I need is to worry about you getting *drunk* while you're traveling alone. What time is it there, young lady? People can take advantage of you."

"One, I haven't been drinking, Mom. Two, I'm not traveling alone, I'm with Collin. The guy I'm marrying. That's why I called."

"You can't be serious," she said after a short silence.

"I am."

Another pause.

"Well, no," she said impassively.

"No what?" I asked. "There was no *yes-or-no* question."

"No, you're not doing that. Don't be ridiculous, Sarah. You come from an important family."

"What does that mean?" I asked, laughing. "Collin's dad's a doctor, and Collin's got a—he's successful, Mom. I don't even feel the need to defend that. He's extremely successful."

"It doesn't matter how successful he is. I've never even met him, Sarah Lynn, and you've only known him for—"

"We're doing it in like ten or twelve days," I said, cutting her off. "I'm a grown woman, Mom, and I'm getting married. I would love your help and your blessing, and I'd love for you to be here, but I'm—"

"Absolutely *not* young lady!" she said with utter scorn. "Your father told me that you were gonna go get drunk in a pub and come home married, and I laughed. I laughed, Sarah. I laughed because it was a *joke*! Your father was *joking*, and we both had a good laugh."

"Well, maybe he said it because he knows how much I like Collin."

"He doesn't know anything about Collin, because *he's never met him*!"

I could not stop tears from flowing out of my eyes. I was exhausted and prone to crying anyway, but my mother's relentless disapproval put me over-the-top. Hot tears ran down my cheeks. I was silent as they fell. I knew if I spoke, my voice would come out high-pitched and barely there, so I stayed quiet.

"Get some rest and call me in the morning when you come to your senses, Sarah."

"I don't want to hang up right now, Mom, because you don't think I'm serious about this, and I am."

"I can hear that you're serious, honey, but I also know that it is a mistake." She said the word *mistake* with contempt, pronouncing every syllable with emphasis.

"Are you saying you won't come?"

She scoffed. "Won't come?" she asked. "Does it *surprise* you that I'm not going to just stop my life and run halfway across the world to witness my daughter go all haywire on me?"

"Haywire? Really?"

"What did you think I would say, Sarah? *Sounds great, why don't you go ahead and marry this guy I've never met before in my life.*"

I was so upset that I found it difficult to breathe—like there was a stiff wall in my throat blocking me from sucking in or breathing out. Try as I might, I could not stop my face from contorting with tears—frustrated, angry, hurt tears.

I held the phone in front of me and pressed the button to disconnect while my mother was still talking on the other end. I stared at the phone with my heart beating like crazy.

How badly I wish I could erase that entire conversation and try it again. Maybe I had just brought it up the wrong way. Maybe a different approach would have helped. I was scared to tell them, but I really did think they would get over it and learn to see it my way. I honestly assumed our conversation would end with them narrowing down a date and asking about flight arrangements. I was intimidated, but I never expected my mom to be so impassive or rude about it.

It hurt. I would be lying if I said I didn't want my parents approval, and it hurt really bad that my mom was so against my plans. I wondered what my dad was thinking, and I briefly considered calling him before deciding that wouldn't be a good idea.

My emotions were swirling around like crazy when a text came through from my mom.

Mom: "I think we got disconnected. Call me back if you need to, honey, but I think you just need some rest from all the jetlag. Everything's gonna be fine once you sleep it off."

I almost text her back, but I couldn't decide on anything to say. It was hard to think through the tears. *How could what I thought had been the best day ever turn into this?*

I tried to assure myself everything would be fine and that I was just delirious, but I felt a sense of dread at my Mom's disapproval. I was sure that she had talked to my dad, and by now, it was a terrible idea to him as well.

I cried from frustration because I had been so excited about marrying Collin, and now it was tainted with this drama. I felt alone and desperate. I had the key to get into Collin's room. It was sitting on the nightstand, and I stared at it. In that moment, I felt desperate for his touch. I just wanted to feel his arms around me.

I used the bed sheets to wipe the tears from my face before grabbing a few of my things to head for the door. It was only after I had his door open that it hit me that I should probably feel bad about going into his room unannounced. I closed the door quietly behind me but stayed still and quiet as I pulled my phone out to text him from his own living room.

I was typing a text to him that told him I was coming to his room when I heard his deep voice pierce through the darkness. I gasped and took a step back, trying to focus on him.

"You okay?" he asked, for the second time.

"Yeah, I was just texting to tell you I was coming over." I spoke in a soft voice. "I'm fine. It's fine. I just wanted to come over here to talk to you for a minute—"

I felt overwhelmed, so I looked down, putting my fingertips to my forehead in an effort to shield my face. Collin came forward and took me into his arms with no hesitation at all. It was exactly what I wanted to happen. He had on pajama pants, but he was shirtless and I felt the warmth of his body surrounding me.

He had thick, muscular arms and a broad chest, and when I was in proximity with it like that, it was easy not to give a flying flip what my parents said. The thought of my parents made a wave of anxiousness hit me, and I let out a helpless sigh.

Collin held me tightly, running a comforting hand down my back. "What happened?"

I paused for a second. "My mom refused to take me seriously about getting married in Ireland," I said. "I probably shouldn't have called her at two in the morning, but I did, and she said I was crazy—she thought I was drunk."

"We don't have to do it this fast," he said easily.

It sounded so logical coming from him, but it sent a pain through my heart.

Collin put his hands on the sides of my face, forcing me to look at him since I hadn't the whole time I'd been in there. I shyly made eye contact, and he smiled sweetly at me.

"Don't cry," he whispered, using a thumb to wipe at the top of my cheek. "Don't," he repeated when another tear fell from my eyes. "Listen, baby girl, the situation's still very much under control." He pulled me into his arms, and I let the side of my face fall onto his chest. He used a hand to hold me there. "You have to forgive them, remember?" he asked, his deep voice sounding even deeper since my ear was against his chest.

I nodded that I knew I needed to forgive them.

"No really," he said. "She's just trying to be a good mom by telling you this isn't a good idea."

"Yeah, but she's wrong," I said. "And now she's gonna miss out, or cause drama, or both."

"Forgiveness, Sarah. Not just for her, but for you. It'll help you think straight. Think about when we have a little girl, and one day she grows up. Wouldn't you feel a little weird if our little girl called you from Ireland and said she was marrying a guy you'd never even met? It'd be hard to hear even if he *was* an amazing young entrepreneur."

I giggled and shook my head before leaning up to place a kiss on his neck, right below his jaw.

"The bad part is that after everything, I still want to do it. I want to go ahead with it whether they approve of it or not. Do your parents approve?"

He shrugged. "I figured I'd call them tomorrow, but I know they'll be happy. I've never done anything like this before, so they'll know I'm serious."

"Well, *I've* never done anything like this before either," I said, assuming that's what he meant.

He chuckled. "I wasn't saying you have, I just know my parents would be onboard, that's all." He rubbed my back again. "But listen, I won't even tell them yet. That'll give us time to talk to your parents and figure things out. I don't want you to be anxious, though, because it's gonna be fine."

"I know, but I wish it could be fine now. Are there words you can say to win them over?" I asked.

"Yes," he said confidently.

"Can you do it?"

"Once I meet them, yes I can. They just have to see how much I love you. That's all they want to know. And who can blame them?"

"Me," I said. "I can blame them because I tried to tell them that. I told Mom I knew what I was doing, and she just wouldn't trust me."

Collin pulled back and tilted my chin up so that I would look at him. "I promise it's gonna be all right," he whispered with an easy smile.

"Can I still marry you?"

"Yes."

"Soon?"

"Yes."

"In Dublin?" I asked.

"If you want to."

"I do."

He smiled. "Then you can."

"If I call my mom, will you say 'hi' to her?" I asked.

His smile grew. "Right now?"

I nodded. "Would you? To know you is to love you, and I just want her to experience that. We'll want our daughter's gorgeous, sweet, smart, entrepreneur boyfriend to do the same for us when she calls us from Ireland."

Chapter 17

I wanted nothing more than to ride off into the sunset with Collin, and I hated the seed of doubt my mother planted in my mind. I had never been more certain of anything in my life, and it hurt that my parents didn't trust me enough to know I wouldn't jump into something this crazy if I didn't know I was meant to be with Collin. He was right when he said that I needed to forgive my mom and try to put myself in her shoes, but I still felt unsettled about the whole situation.

Collin pulled me into his bedroom. There was a T-shirt on the edge of his bed, and I followed him in there, watching in awe as he put it on. I shamelessly gawked as he stretched it above his head and pulled it, first onto his arms and then over his head and chest. It was like watching an underwear ad, and I glanced away just to lessen the tensing reaction in my abdomen.

"I'm not promising a miracle," he said referring to calling my mother. "But I'll try my best."

"You don't have to do it if you don't want to," I said. "I want you to, but I understand if it's weird."

"It's not weird." He flashed his perfectly white teeth at me. "Anything?" he asked (wondering if he had anything stuck between them).

I smiled and shook my head, and watched as he ran a hand through his hair.

"What are you doing?"

"I thought we'd Facetime," he said. "You think she's up for it?" He glanced at the clock, and I could see his wheels turning as he tried to remember what time it was in New York.

"She's up," I said. "I just talked to her. Would you seriously do that?"

"Yep." He smiled and looked down at his own chest. "Otherwise why would I get dressed?"

"Because I came in," I said, checking him out and biting at my bottom lip.

He squinted his eyes at me like I should know better than to say such a thing. "You can see me without my shirt on, baby girl. You're my fiancé."

I smiled and reached out to pinch at him.

"Go ahead and call your mama," he said, pulling me to the couch so we could sit next to each other.

We flopped into our respective seats, and I felt so relieved and protected that I reached over and put a kiss on his cheek before dialing my mom's number.

"This better be good, Sarah Lynn" I heard her say when she picked up. Her camera was facing the ceiling fan in her bedroom instead of where I could see her.

"What are you doing?" I asked, holding my end of the camera onto a random place on the wall instead of at my face. Two can play that game.

"I was reading, and your father's watching an episode of his own show on television."

"Is he right there?" I asked. My mom's end of the camera moved, and I watched as her face came into view. She followed herself as she leaned to her right, letting my father come into view as well.

"Hey Dad," I said. I aimed my phone at myself, being careful not to include Collin in the picture just yet.

"Hey sweetheart," Dad said. "You've got your mother all nervous over here."

"Oh yeah?"

"Uh-huh," he said.

She held the camera out, aiming it at both of them, and I watched as my dad turned down the television.

"Collin's right here," I said quietly. My heart felt like it might explode with anticipation, and I pleaded with myself to calm down and speak clearly. "I wanted to straighten things out with you guys for two reasons. First, because I'm actually marrying Collin, and I couldn't sleep without you guys knowing that for sure and maybe even being okay with it. Second, I really want you to come here. I want you to be here for it. I don't ask you guys for much, but I'm—"

"Sarah, you cannot be serious," my mom said.

"Can I say something?" Collin asked.

His question was directed at me since the camera wasn't even aimed at him, but my parents heard him make the request; I could tell by my mom's stunned expression.

"I'm gonna put Collin on, okay?"

Mom huffed and began adjusting her hair as if Collin hadn't been able to see her the whole time, which he had. I aimed the camera at Collin, and my mother treated it like he was seeing her for the first time and not the other way around.

I just sat there, a big bundle of nerves, waiting to hear what they would say.

"Hey Mrs. Spicer, Mr. Spicer," Collin said with a genuine smile and wave.

"Hello there," my dad said.

And at the same time, my mom said, "Hi, Collin," with a little more motherly enthusiasm.

Collin took a deep breath as he regarded each of them on the screen. I wanted to jump in and say something to fill every little break in conversation, but I refrained from doing so, choosing instead to sit back and let them talk.

"I know it must seem hard to believe that we would want to get married this soon after we met each other," Collin said, skipping the small talk.

"Yes it does," my dad agreed with a straight face.

"I know our circumstances aren't what you'd consider normal."

"That's an understatement," my dad interjected, drawing a patient smile from Collin.

"I truly love your daughter, Mr. Spicer. I know you guys only want what's best for her, and I'm thankful for that. I'm glad she has people in her life that have her best interest in mind. I respect you for assuming this is a bad idea. I really do appreciate where you're coming from. But I have to tell you, you're wrong this time."

"And what would be *right*?" my dad asked, still scowling. "Giving you two my blessing?"

"Yes sir," Collin said. "I know it must not feel right, but it is. If I could somehow stare into this camera just the right way to tell you how much I love her, I would do it. If I could somehow let you see directly into my innermost feelings and intentions, I would do it. I would let you see that my number one goal is to protect her and not harm her. But as it stands all I can do is sit here and let you look at me on a computer screen and tell you thank you for raising such a precious daughter. Sarah would not be who she is today without you two, and I feel like I owe you something for that. I know how amazing she is, and I'm too smart and determined to let her go." Collin paused and gave them a sincere smile. "Both of us are patient people," he added. "We understand perfectly that we have options... that by all standards we should hold off a little while before we decide to get married."

"Exactly," my mom said. "Thank you."

Collin gave her a smile that was edged with regret. "That's the thing," he said with a little remorse. "We're not waiting. Neither of us cares about the status quo." He smiled sincerely at them. "I love your daughter. I want to take care of her and come home to her. I want to know you guys and have you know my family. It's gonna be all good, and you'll just have to see that once we stay together." He paused to sigh and smile at me before he faced them again. "That being said, we've decided to get married, and that's what we're doing. We both like the idea of doing it here in Ireland, so that's how it's shaping up."

My parents just sat there, staring at us with unreadable expressions. I had no idea what they were thinking. "This is all a bit hard to believe," my mom said, finally.

"It's crazy for me, too, if you want to know the truth," Collin said. "If you had told me a month ago that I'd be saying something like this to a girl's parents, I wouldn't have believed you, but here we are. Life surprises you sometimes." He smiled at me and wrapped his arm around my shoulder before focusing on them again. "And when it does, you hop on a six-hour flight from JFK to Dublin to celebrate with your daughter and the man who loves her."

We all stared at each other for a few silent seconds.

"I need to give this to my writers," my dad said, with a serious expression. He looked down his nose, through his reading glasses as if to check something on the device. "Did this thing record what he just said?" he asked my mom. "Ethan's character is gonna get married, and he needs to say that speech to Sydney's family." He looked at Collin with an earnest expression. "Could you say it again? Have you ever thought about acting?"

"Honey," my mom pleaded. "This isn't a TV show, it's real life. Do you understand he's not acting? He's telling you he wants to marry our daughter."

My dad and mom were looking at each other when he said, "Yes, I do realize what he's saying, honey, and I went from planning a way to rescue my daughter to feeling like I wanted to hug the man. I'm already making travel arrangements in my head." Dad paused and gestured toward the screen with an amazed expression. "I mean, I think he loves her. I'm convinced. That's why I'm trying to remember that whole speech. Do you think it recorded?"

"He does love me," I said, holding the screen onto my face like I was hugging them before pulling back again. "That's why he convinced you, because he really does."

I knew by their expressions that Collin had won them over (or at least softened them considerably), so I took advantage of that.

"I know it's late. It's way later here. Thank you so much for being on board. I'm gonna sleep better tonight knowing you guys are coming. Love you! We'll talk tomorrow and figure everything out. Bye, love you!"

I waved and smiled as I reached for the button to disconnect, while still giving them enough time to interject if they had any major objections. They said nothing, just waved and smiled with matching stunned expressions, which I knew meant they were coming to Ireland. I was smirking at my dad's face when I pressed the button to disconnect.

"Oh, my gosh, we're gonna do this," I said.

"Yep," he said, taking me into his arms so quickly that I squealed. "Come on, I couldn't sleep either." He pulled me toward the bedroom. "I have the TV on in here, and I want you next to me." He pulled off his shirt and tossed it onto the foot of the bed before climbing in. He gave me a toss of the head to tell me to follow him, and he turned down the covers next to him, indicating that it was my spot. "Come on," he said. "I'm not gonna touch you or even kiss you. I just want you next to me."

I was planning on going before he even said that, and I ran and hopped onto the bed, rolling into my place, only I overshot it a little and had to catch myself from falling completely off the other side. Actually, Collin was the one who caught me. He reached out and grabbed me as I pounced and rolled.

I longed to be next to him so badly that the act of stretching out beside him, made me instantly sleepy and subdued. Relaxation washed over me. I had never loved anyone so much in my whole life, nor had I ever been this comfortable.

"I love you," I said stretching out next to him.

"I know," he said.

"How?"

"Because I'm smart, and I can tell. I can see what people are into me for, and you're into me for me." He paused as if choosing his words. "You see past everything I have, right down to the inside of me, and you still love me. You forgive me for things I haven't even done yet, and that just makes me want to never do anything to disappoint you. I love you like a fat kid loves popsicles."

I laughed. "*I, I love you like a love song, baby,*" I sang in my best sleepy Selena Gomez impression.

Collin tickled me for that, which made me giggle and end up even closer to him. I fit myself next to him, lining up our curves just right, and when I glanced up to meet his gaze, our faces were almost touching.

"I'm not gonna kiss you," he whispered.

Our lips were only about two three inches apart. I could feel his breath when he spoke. He smiled at my disappointed expression.

"What? If I kiss you now while we're here in this comfortable bed, I'll end up trying to talk you into other things. Just lay beside me and help me not to ravish you before we get married."

I leaned toward him placing my mouth right next to his ear. "I want to be ravished so bad," I whispered. I pulled back to see that his eyes were closed. He pinched them closed more tightly before finally opening them to smile at me.

"Here's what's gonna happen," he said. "There will be no more ear-whispering tonight. You're gonna lay by me, and I'm gonna to lay by you, and we'll watch TV until we both fall asleep. And tomorrow and the next day, we're going to get up and be tourists in Ireland. I'm gonna buy you a ring to put on your finger, and introduce you as my soon-to-be wife, but I'm not going to kiss you again until you're all mine."

"Seriously? That's so long!"

"It's really not," he said sweetly. "Besides, you waited this long. It's not every day you meet a bride who gets a white wedding."

"It's real gentlemanly of you to think of me and my morals and everything, but really, what's up with the no kissing thing?" I asked sleepily as I nestled my head into the pillow next to him.

He turned and shifted to get it just right as he settled in next to me. "It's just a few days," he said. "I think it'll be fun—it'll give us something to look forward to."

"It's gonna be super hard," I said, my voice sounding sleepier and sleepier with every passing second.

"Yeah, but just imagine how fun it'll be when I marry you," he said, sounding sleepy and unsure as he patted me on the shoulder. "I'm just gonna turn off the TV," he added, noticing that both of us were spent.

"Uh-huh," I said. "Night, love you."

He pressed the button on the remote and the room went dark. I couldn't think of a single thing that would make me any more comfortable than I was right then.

"Night," he said. "Love you."

Okay, maybe that little phrase was the one thing capable of making me even cozier than I already was. I smiled at the thought as I drifted off to sleep.

Chapter 18

If I had to construct a montage, a collection of memories, from those days in Dublin with Collin, it would consist of laughing, dancing, talking, eating, walking, snuggling, holding hands, and sightseeing. One afternoon, we rented a luxury sports car and went for a drive in the country. And another day, we rode around Dublin on a scooter. I had never laughed so much in my life. Collin was never completely away from his work, but he contained it to a few hours each day, which meant we were hanging out most of the time.

We had countless moments where we would stare at each other, knowing we could both feel the extent of our love. We smiled knowingly at one another every time we figured out something else we had in common. We did all of those things repeatedly, and yet there was *still no kissing*.

For three days, we spent almost every waking moment with each other, knowing full well how very in love we were, yet not kissing at all. Not once. He held my hand, and that was the extent of our contact. I even canceled my room and snuggled up next to him in the bed every night, and he still didn't try anything. He wore a T-shirt to sleep for goodness sake.

Honestly, it just made me want him more. It was the first time in my life that I felt like my role had been reversed with a guy, and I quite liked it. Maybe Collin knew that, and that's why he was doing it. Either way, it worked. I absolutely couldn't wait till I got to kiss his lips again.

Thankfully, I would not have to wait much longer since this was finally the day. It had been a week since Collin left for London, and today was the day I would become his wife. He would be coming back to Dublin today at noon, which would give him two hours to get to the estate and wrap his mind around saying 'I do'. He might have preferred a day or two in Dublin to get settled and chill out before the wedding, but it didn't work out that way. On such short notice, we easily narrowed it down to the nearest Sunday, which was a day that worked out for everyone involved, including the Steiners who graciously agreed to let us use their house.

Their estate was the epitome of old-world elegance, and they rolled out the red carpet for us since they loved my dad and were fans of Collin's. There simply weren't houses like this in America— at least I have never been in any of them. It was a manor. I half expected people to be wearing period clothing.

Between my family and Collin's, and a few select friends, we flew 18 people in from the states. We ended up inviting a few others we had met in Ireland, including John and Ellen, and the barkeeper, Luke. Collin had a few he was bringing from

London as well, so there were just over 30 of us in all, and most everyone was already there.

It was a beautiful, slightly cool day, and we planned on having a short, simple ceremony in the main courtyard before spending the afternoon together in sort of an extended reception. The Steiners loved to host and were extremely gracious about welcoming our guests into their beautiful home. Some of them were even staying a night or two there before heading back to the states.

They had drawing rooms and sitting rooms with all sorts of parlor games, and as part of the celebration, they planned on entertaining everyone for the entire afternoon before feeding us dinner that evening. Collin offered to take care of the catering, but they insisted they would do it so he could relax and enjoy his wedding. The Steiner's had taken care of literally everything.

I overheard my father telling my mom he would end up reimbursing them, but neither of my parents said anything to me about money or the trouble it had taken to get the whole family over to Ireland in a week's notice.

Lu came, and so did one of my childhood friends named Emily. Drake also came not only as my friend, but also as our hired photographer. He had already taken what seemed like a thousand pictures of me since I arrived at the Steiner's house.

"What time is it?" I asked, looking at myself in the mirror. I was styled in a way that fit the house with a soft, flowy, empire-waist gown and my hair down and in waves. I had a simple wreath of flowers around my head with a thin white veil attached to it.

"Thirty minutes till show time," Drake said, glancing at his watch before pointing the camera at me again.

"It looks like everyone's already here," my mom said, looking through a nearby window, which let her see an area where everyone was gathered.

"Most of them are," Mrs. Steiner said in her thick Irish brogue as she entered the room. Her husband was American, but she was Irish through and through, which was why they had ended up back in Dublin. "I was asked to give ya this," she said, offering me a piece of paper. Mrs. Steiner was soft spoken, so I hadn't really heard exactly what she said, but I took the folded piece of paper and opened it, barely aware of the fact that Drake was snapping photos of me.

It was a handwritten note that simply said:

Follow Mrs. Steiner, my love.

I read the words, and my head whipped up to look at Mrs. Steiner who was standing there with an innocent expression. "I guess yer comin' wi me, then," she whispered.

"Where are we going?" I asked.

"To the place where Collin tole me to take ya."

"So, I just follow you?" I asked, glancing around at the ladies who were expecting me to stay in this one stationary location until I walked into the courtyard to marry Collin.

"Yes, ma'am, I do believe that's what he wants." She gestured for me to follow her and I did so with no further questions.

I was already out of my mind with nerves, and now it was even worse. Collin and I had already talked about not seeing each other before the ceremony, and I couldn't imagine why he would change his mind. It was difficult not to assume the worst.

"No photos, please," Mrs. Steiner said when she saw that Drake was following us.

"Really?" he asked.

"Right," she said with a nod. "Collin specifically said he didn't want her bein' followed."

Drake and I shared a somewhat worried expression as he hesitated but ultimately decided to stay behind.

"Don't worry, lass, I think he just wants to talk to ya," Mrs. Steiner said as I followed her down the long, empty corridor that led away from the main area of the house.

"Where are we going?" I asked.

"To the west garden."

"What's over there?" I asked.

She glanced at me with a little smile. "Collin."

She reached out and opened the wooden door that led outside. We were under a series of stone awnings, and I could see the stone wall around what

I knew to be the west garden since I had already taken some pictures out there.

"Is he coming out here?" I asked when Mrs. Steiner stood at the door, looking like she was leaving me to it.

"He's already over there," she said. She gestured to the stone wall, and I looked at it again, seeing nothing. "Jus go over there. He's waitin' for ya."

"Thank you," I said with a nod as Mrs. Steiner smiled and closed the door.

I walked toward the wall, feeling more anxious than ever. I knew in my heart it wasn't the case, but I couldn't stop the thought from crossing my mind that Collin might be dragging me out there to dump me. My heart was singing, and pounding, and aching, and breaking—all at the same time.

"Hello?" I said.

"Pssssst," I heard.

Just the playfulness of the sound made me smile.

"Pssst," I said back.

"Come here," he said.

I walked toward the sound of his voice, knowing it was coming from the other side of the wall.

"I don't want you to see me," I said. I put my hands on the wall, knowing in my heart that I was close to the place where he was on the other side.

"Pssst," I heard him say again.

The sound was coming from a nearby crack in the wall. There was a hole, letting in light from the other side, and I had just spotted it when two fingers came out, wiggling to catch my attention. I gasped and instantly reached out to touch him, smiling uncontrollably. I missed him so badly that it felt like a miracle to finally touch his flesh. I grabbed his fingers, feeling like I wanted to pull him all the way through that hole like a comical cartoon bunny who was tugging a carrot out of the ground. I needed to get to him so badly that I wanted to cry. I held onto his fingers with one hand, while my other hand was glued to the wall, like maybe if I wished hard enough, the heavy stones would break to bits, and I could get to Collin.

"I changed my mind about kissing you," he said, sounding a little impatient.

I hadn't really had the chance to consider his whole statement, because it began with, *I changed my mind*, which was a red flag phrase for a bride on her wedding day.

"What did you change your mind about?" I asked, knowing he had said more.

"Kissing you," he said. "I don't want to wait."

"Well you have to," I said, "because you can't see me before we go out there. It's tradition."

"I won't look at you. I just want to kiss you. I don't want to wait for the wedding, because I don't want to share it with anyone. I don't want anyone taking our picture, and I don't want you thinking about what anyone else thinking. I want your lips on mine, Sarah. I won't look at you, but I brought you out here to kiss you, and that's what I intend to do."

"What if I say no?" I asked, knowing I would never do that since I was feeling absolutely desperate to kiss him.

"And why would ya do that?" he asked with an Irish accent.

"I wouldn't," I said.

Before I knew what was happening, Collin shoved a strip of fabric through the hole in the fence, and I tugged on it, pulling roughly an arm's length of fabric out of the hole before inspecting it curiously.

"It's from the curtains, I think," he explained. "I told Mrs. Steiner about our little predicament, and she's said these would work."

"You told Mrs. Steiner?"

"Yes, love, she's the one who brought you the note. Come stand over here by the gate, and tie it around your eyes. I will find you, and my lips will find yours, and then we will pretend this never happened and go get married."

I had already taken two steps to the big wooden gate, and tied my blindfold by the time he finished his speech. I wanted to touch him so badly that if he hadn't come up with some kind of plan, I probably would have burst through the wall. I heard the gate open, and I put my hand on the edge of the doorway.

"My hand's in the door, so don't close it," I said.

Collin must've taken that has a clue, because seconds later, his hand was on mine. In a quick burst of movement, we found each other blindly and I fell into his arms, holding him around his middle, and feeling so grateful to finally touch him, smell him. We held onto each other with equal fervor, squeezing and fitting our bodies together.

We stayed like that for several long seconds before he pulled back and began finding my face with his hands. I felt him blindly but gently grope for the sides of my face, which he situated between both of his hands.

He put his mouth ever so close to mine. I could not see him, but he was so close that I could feel it there. It was a thrilling feeling, knowing I was about to be kissed, but unable to see anything at all.

"How do I know it's you?" I whispered breathlessly.

"I assure you," he whispered, "I would *not* let any one else be doing this to you right now."

His mouth was so close to mind that I could feel his words.

"Why, because I'm yours?" I asked.

"Uh-huh."

"In a minute, I'm gonna be Mrs. Ross," I said.

"I know."

"I love you, Collin."

He leaned even closer closing the gap completely. "I (kiss) love (kiss) you (longer, lingering kiss)."

He pulled back a little after those three kisses, and I gave a little whimper, letting him know I was sad to feel him go.

"No one gets to share this one with us," he whispered. He put his lips on mine again, and I responded by stretching up to meet him. Collin turned my head in his hands and kissed me deeply. He kissed me like he had never kissed me before. He kissed me in a way that conveyed so much more than just physical attraction. He showed me I was his, and in those all-too-brief seconds, I gave myself over to the passion and emotion of it all.

We were both breathless when he pulled away. I couldn't see him, of course, but I could hear us breathing, and could tell by our movements that we were both working to catch our breath.

"Go," he said, reluctantly. "Give me five seconds to get this gate closed before you take off your blindfold. I'll see you at our wedding."

Chapter 19

While I wasn't sure I would ever, in my life, tell someone I'd been "*kissed silly*," it was the only way to explain what Collin had just done to me in the garden. He kissed me silly, and I walked from the garden into the house, feeling stunned and delirious from it.

I entered the house, and made my way down the long hallway to the room where I knew I'd find Lu and my mom, and perhaps even Drake. I was still holding the strip of fabric when I came in, and everyone spotted it right away. I must not have anticipated them noticing it, because it took me by surprise when they did.

"What's that?" my mom asked.

"Fabric," I said, casually.

"What'd he want?" Drake asked, still looking curious about the whole no photograph thing.

"He just wanted to ask me something," I said, looking as innocent as I could. I realized that my lips were probably still a little swollen from the massive kiss, and I puckered and shifted my mouth to draw attention away from it, although I might have accomplished the opposite.

Thinking about my puffy lips made me try to remember whether Collin was clean-shaven or not. My senses were on overload from kissing him blindfolded, and I could honestly not say whether I thought he was clean-shaven or not. The thought put a smile on my face.

"What happened?" my mom asked. "Are you pregnant or something?"

Her words made my daydream come to a screeching halt. "What? Mom, no."

"Did you *see* him?" Lu asked with wide eyes.

"No," I said.

"Then why are you grinning like that?" Lu asked.

Snap, snap, snap, went the camera, recording still shots of the whole conversation.

"I'm not," I said.

I looked directly at the camera and squinted my eyes at Drake. *Snap.* I made a comical scowl, and there was yet another *snap, snap,* causing the women in the room to laugh. I was so crazy in love with Collin that I didn't even care if they figured out what I had just done.

Everyone besides Lu and my mom went outside with the other guests. They seemed to both realize I had a lot going on mentally, because they were content to just talk to each other while helping me make the last-minute touches on my makeup.

My mom had a ton of questions for Lu about Shower & Shelter, and Lu was excited to answer them. The Netflix documentary was apparently moving forward, and they were talking about making Lu one of their subjects since they were looking to start in August, and that's specifically when she would be the new recruit. They were still in the very early stages, and Lu's place in the production wasn't set in stone, but the producers had contacted her within the last week, and she was obviously elated about it.

The plan was to follow the lives of five of the S&S artists (and of course the gallery in general). They would shoot the documentary over the period of roughly a year, checking in and spending time with each artist on a weekly basis. Lu was thrilled about the possibility, especially because it would come with a twenty-thousand-dollar paycheck for her trouble.

I enjoyed hearing about it, and so did my mom, and it was a welcome distraction from how very over the moon nervous I was.

"It's beautiful out here," Lu said as she pulled me toward the courtyard. "You're going to love it."

"Slow down," my mom said from my other side. "You don't want to be winded by the time you get out there."

Mrs. Steiner was in the main hall when we made our way in that direction. "Come on," she said, holding her hand out for me. I gave her a curious expression, which she ignored. She looked at my mom and Lu. "Ye two go out that way," she said. "Ye'll see where they saved ye a spot." She looked at me. "Yer comin' wi me."

My mom and Lu took off, and Mrs. Steiner grabbed me by the hand.

"Where are we going? "I asked. I was convinced that Collin was up to one last piece of mischief, and my heart started racing. "Where are we going?" I repeated.

"Upstairs," she said. "Everyone's expecting you to enter from up there."

I knew exactly what staircase she was talking about, but I had no idea I was using it. No one had told me this part when we rehearsed. She pulled me up a set of interior stairs, and we made our way down a huge, second-story hallway before she stopped at a set of French doors.

"Everyone's on the other side," she said. "You'll see them down below in the courtyard. I'm gonna open the door for ye, but I'm steppin' out of the way as soon as I do."

I glanced at her with a terrified expression, and she smiled sweetly at me.

"You look bonnie, Sarah, and all the lovely people on the other side of the door here are just here because they love ya."

I gave her a little smile as I took a deep calming breath.

"Okay, now it's gonna be bright when I open the door because the sun's comin' down right here. Just know that ye have about ten feet of patio before ye get to the stairs. Ye'll take the stairs on yer own, and ye'll see yer dad waitin' at the bottom. He'll walk ye to Collin. Got it?"

I nodded even though I didn't have it. I had only partially heard what she said. I barely even had time to nod when Mrs. Steiner thrust a handful of wildflowers into my hand and reached in front of me, opening the door and letting sunlight come streaming onto my face.

I held my hand in front of my eyes to shield some of the bright sun as I stepped onto the sprawling, stone patio. I was still letting my eyes adjust when I heard one of those two-toned whistles that someone did when they appreciated how good someone looked. The high-pitched sound most definitely came from my brother, Joe, who was prone to lighten the mood by doing such things. I loved that it gave me an excuse to smile as I crossed the upstairs terrace headed for the stairs. I grinned at my brother's whistle until I came to the edge of the stairs and tried to focus on the people below.

My gaze fell on the back edge of the crowd first, and I saw some of Collin's colleagues along with the new friends we met in Ireland. I scanned the crowd, finding my family and Collin's family. I stood at the edge of the staircase taking it all in—the beautiful courtyard and the thirty or so sharply dressed people who were all there because they loved me.

It was the thought of being loved that made me remember to find Collin. Somehow, in the rush of it all, I thought he wasn't out there yet, but I searched for him the instant I remembered he was.

My eyes shot to the center of the courtyard where I knew he'd be standing, and sure enough, there he was. His face broke into a grin the instant he saw that I found him, and I smiled back, feeling crazy for taking so much time looking at everyone else.

Collin was standing there in a dashing, navy blue suit. He was immaculately dressed from his slicked-back hair to his tan, wingtip shoes. There was a lot of space between us, and I wanted it gone immediately. He was exactly what my eyes wanted to see. If I could have only had one time in my whole life where I blinked and ended up in a different location, it would be now, and I would go from where I was to where he was.

I was so desperate to go to him that I picked up my dress and started trotting down the staircase. I was wearing a formal white gown, but underneath were my favorite pair of red low-top Chuck Taylors. I vaguely heard the crowd responding to either the site of them or the sight of me running down the stairs, but I only had one thing on my mind, and that was getting to Collin.

I jogged as carefully as I could, praying I didn't do a face plant in front of everyone. My dad was standing at the bottom of the stairs, and I stopped briefly to talk to him. I smiled and kissed him on the cheek, knowing he'd go along with whatever I said.

"I love you, Daddy, but I got it from here. I'm running to him."

He gave me a loving smile that meant I should go, and I didn't hesitate to do just that. I left my dad at the foot of those stairs and started out toward Collin at a much faster pace than I would have been going had I been walking with my dad.

Collin didn't stay put either. Once he saw that I had left my dad in favor of running toward him, he started toward me as well. We met about twenty feet away from where we were supposed to wind up, but I didn't even give that a second thought because the next thing I knew, I was in Collin's arms.

He caught me, spinning me around to carry my momentum before we came to a breathless stop right there in the aisle. We paid no attention to the people around us or the fact that we were standing in the wrong spot. He looked at me, and I looked at him, and we both knew what a relief it was to finally get to see each other.

I smiled and shook my head absentmindedly, thinking of how gorgeous he looked out there in the sunlight with his suit on. He smiled back at me, and without pausing to think better of it, I stretched up and kissed him right on the mouth. It wasn't a quick, accidental kiss, either. I wrapped my hand around the back of his head and held him there, letting our mouths meet while we stared right into each other's eyes.

My brother started with a whistle and then the entire group burst into applause. Collin smiled and kissed me again before taking me by the hand to lead me back to the spot where he had been standing before.

Neither of us had anyone standing next to us. It was just Collin, the priest, and me, and all of our guests sat on stone benches and in extra chairs that had been placed nearby. We had a simple ceremony that only lasted about ten minutes. The priest said a few things and so did Collin. He spoke about the circumstances of how we met and how from the first moment he saw me, he knew I was his sunshine. He told them how much he cared for me, and somehow in the midst of it, he recited his vows.

My part wasn't as eloquent as Collin's, and the priest led me through my vows, but I had written them from the heart, and I felt like everything I said went well with Collin's speech. Plus, I had already promised to just be comfortable, natural, and true to myself so that I didn't regret any part of this day. It didn't matter what everyone else thought of the ceremony; it just mattered that Collin and I were telling each other the truth, and we were... I could feel it.

Collin kissed me again at the end of the ceremony, and this time it was different. This time he was kissing Mrs. Ross. I knew I had done the right thing by marrying him, and felt like happiness might come oozing right out of me.

Everyone was still cheering for us after he kissed me, and he leaned down to speak into my ear.

"Do we have to spend the whole afternoon entertaining these people?" he asked. He was talking to me, but he said it loud enough that I was sure the priest heard.

"Yes," I said.

He pulled back and stared at me, looking at me like he wanted to eat me alive. "Why would we do that?"

I giggled, feeling delighted at his impatience. "Because everyone wants to hang out with us," I said, trying to look like I was fine with waiting, even though I wasn't."

The priest had already introduced us once, but he did it again since Collin and I seemed content to just stand there and have a conversation with each other.

He sweetly (and for the second time) introduced us as *Mr. and Mrs. Ross* in his thick Irish accent, and Collin and I peeled our eyes off of each other with great difficulty so that we could face the crowd and wave at everyone.

Chapter 20

Mr. Steiner gave a speech right after our ceremony. He thanked everyone for being there explained what parts of the house were open and prepared for guests with refreshments, music, and games. A formal dinner was to be served promptly at 6.

I knew everyone (including our new Irish friends) would be staying through until dinner because Mrs. Steiner had everyone RSVP so that her chef would know how many he would need to serve.

None of this was my idea. Mrs. Steiner had taken it upon herself to host our wedding and reception in the way she chose, and honestly, I was relieved to not have to deal with it since I knew absolutely nothing about planning weddings.

I must say I was a bit surprised when my mom informed me that the Steiners wanted to make it an afternoon-long ordeal. They thought it would be nice since our families had traveled all that way. They were eager hosts, so I ended up just putting it in their hands and telling myself that I'd be happy with it no matter what it was. I was completely right to trust them. The Steiners made me feel like a complete princess the whole time, and I was humbled that they acted like it was their honor to do so.

It was truly a fairytale day. There was traditional Irish music in the main hall with a 4-piece band, consisting of guitar, accordion, fiddle, and flute. The guy on guitar also did a lot of stomping, so maybe that made him the drummer, too.

There was a huge fireplace in the billiards room, along with couches and tables, making it one of the most popular locations for the party guests to hang out, only second to the main hall where the band was playing. Then some genius in the group asked the band to move into the billiards room. It was large enough to accommodate our whole party, so for the rest of the afternoon we all pretty much stayed in that one location, laughing and dancing, and just sitting around talking.

There wasn't a single person in the place who looked like they were having a bad time. Not that I wouldn't forgive them if they did because I already decided that some level of drama would be a possibility, and I knew ahead of time I would forgive the culprit if it came to that.

All that pre-drama forgiveness, and there was no need to forgive anyone after all. Everyone had the time of their lives, and if they didn't, then they were all great actors, because it sure seemed like they were pleased as punch about our marriage and thrilled to be in Dublin to celebrate it.

The Steiners had a huge dining table like the ones you'd imagine in medieval days. It was large enough to easily accommodate all of our guests. Mr. Steiner sat on one end of it, and Collin on the other, and we all took our designated places—me of course, positioned right next to Collin. The table was huge, and I felt far away from him, so I scooted my chair closer to the end so that I could hold his hand.

We made conversation with those sitting right around us, but several times during the meal someone would clang a fork to their glass to get everyone's attention so that they could give a speech. My dad gave one, Collin's dad gave one, and my brothers shared one where Eli started to give his own, and Joe wound up interrupting in a sweet but jovial way that had everyone laughing.

Collin said a few words after that, and before I knew it, there was an empty cup where my tea had been and my mostly-eaten dessert was sitting in front of me.

I now heard talk of the evening being over. Everyone went on and on about what an amazing time they had and helped us thank the Steiners for welcoming us into their home. We had begun to stir in a way that made it apparent the meal was over.

I leaned over to speak to Collin. "This dinner took forever," I said.

He smiled. "I know. At least it seems that way to us since we... have other plans and everything."

"I've definitely got other plans," I said.

"You do?"

I nodded. "You want to know what I'm doing in about five minutes?" I asked.

"What?" he asked, still grinning at me.

I put my mouth near his ear. "I'm takin' my new husban to bed," I said. "I've got a new outfit for it and everythin." I had gone over the words in my head at least ten times before I said them to him. I knew the accent would sound good. I had been around Dubliners for almost two weeks now, and I was much better at making myself sound Irish and not like a pirate.

"What did you say?" he asked, pulling back to stare at me.

I smiled and repeated the whole phrase in his ear, not even flinching about delivering the accent.

Collin stood up so quickly that it startled me.

His chair screeched on the ground as he shot to his feet, pulling me up with him and clearing his throat to get everyone's attention. I thought about the speed in which he moved when I said those words, and it made me feel tickled. I giggled and sank my face into his chest, knowing everyone was now looking at us.

"I just want you all to know that we've had an amazing time spending the day with all of you..." Collin paused, and my brother cut in.

"But see ya later," Joe said.

"Exactly!" Collin said, pointing at my brother with wide eyes like he was thankful to have it said in those words.

This caused everyone to laugh.

"Are you guys in a hurry?" my mom asked in a disappointed tone from her place at the table.

And in unison, every single one of the men at the table (save my dad) said, "*Yes!*"

Collin waved and bowed as he began making his way toward the door, taking me with him. I followed easily since that's what I wanted him to do. I couldn't wait to get out of there. We would spend the next five days in an actual castle, and as far as I was concerned, the sooner we got there the better.

"*Form a tunnel!*" Mrs. Steiner yelled from the end of the table.

Everyone stopped to stare at her with matching surprised expressions because she was normally so soft-spoken.

"Sorry, but weren't we going to throw the rice?"

It took maybe two minutes to round everyone up, but they all went outside in a hurry, grabbing handfuls of this beautiful confetti Drake had bought specifically because he knew it made for a good pictures. It was dark outside, but their beautiful home had spotlights, and yet again I felt like a princess when I walked out and everyone cheered and threw confetti for us.

Our bags were already packed in the sleek black car that was waiting out front, and Collin and I got into the backseat, laughing at the chaos and confetti. He rolled down the window so that I could wave to everyone, and I smiled at the sight of all of them yelling and waving back at us.

Once we were far enough away that no one was waving at us anymore, I plopped back, onto the seat with a long sigh.

"You tired?" he asked.

I sat up, feeling thankful that I was finally able to focus on him and him alone. It was the first time I'd been able to do that all day.

"No," I said with a little shrug. "I was just sighing to sigh, I guess." I looked over my shoulder. "They're all gonna be back in America by the next time I see them," I said.

"Yep. Most of them are headed back in the morning, I think."

"I can't believe they were all here. I mean, even Lu and Emily came."

"You wanna go back?" he asked.

I gave him a puzzled expression, asking if he was serious, and he shrugged.

"I think most of them are spending the night there tonight," he said. "I just thought if you were sad about leaving, we could—"

I cut him off by shaking my head, and I scooted closer to him, nestling in his arm and staring up at him. "I am definitely not sad about leaving," I said. "I'm glad they came and everything, and I'm glad everyone is on their best behavior. I think it went great and I wouldn't trade a minute of it. But, the truth of it is, Mr. Ross, that I was ready for that dinner to be over before it even started." I scooted even closer, putting my face right by his face, and feeling like I couldn't get close enough to him. "I just kept telling myself it would be over soon, and before I knew it, we'd be alone."

"And now look," he said, gesturing to the otherwise empty backseat.

"Not quite," I said, cutting my eyes at the driver who was not paying attention to us at all.

I stayed wrapped in Collin's arms all the way to the castle where we would spend the next five days off the grid, or mostly off the grid. We would probably go into Dublin at least a time or two. And Collin knew he would have to answer a few phone calls for work, but we were mostly each other's for the next five days, and I was ecstatic.

I stared out the window as we drove up to the castle. Even at night, the approach to it was absolutely breathtaking. The whole process of checking in and being shown to our quarters was a surreal experience, and I was relieved to have Collin by my side since he was always confident and sure.

Somehow, making it to our room seemed to take an eternity and, at the same time, a split second. We walked through ancient rooms and down stone hallways before coming to our beautiful suite.

It was done in ornate blues and golds and was one of the most beautiful places I had ever seen. It looked like something you'd see in a coffee table book, or on a movie set. I looked around in awe as we stood near the door.

I glanced over my shoulder, feeling giddy to be behind closed doors with Collin for the first time as his wife. He had already loosened his tie and the first few buttons of his shirt, but he made quick work of kicking off his shoes and unbuttoning his shirt the rest of the way, untucking it as he fiddled with the buttons.

I took a deep breath, scanning the room, and still feeling taken aback by its grandeur. "Where's Drake when we need him?" I said, referring to wanting a picture of the room. I was really just saying anything to distract myself from literally throwing myself at Collin.

"The last thing we need in this room right now is Drake," he said.

I smiled at him. "Is that what I said? I didn't even think about it when it was coming out of my mouth. I was really just saying anything so that you wouldn't know what I was really thinking, which was..."

I was planning on saying something about wanting to be dragged off to bed with some sort of Irish accent, but instead I trailed off. I was feeling confident when I started to say it, but I suddenly got shy. Collin moved to stand next to me in a slow, measured movement as he looked me over appraisingly.

I knew how he was looking at me, and it made my blood turn warm. I felt the need to squirm with joy or anticipation or some measure of both. I could hardly stand still.

"What were you really thinking?" he asked, after taking what seemed like a whole minute to stare at me.

"What?" I asked, feeling short of breath.

He stood right next to me, so close that our bodies were touching. My heart was pounding.

"You said you were trying to distract me from what you were really thinking, and I was asking what that was," he said.

He stood right in front of me, and my downcast eyes fell onto his undershirt, which was still tucked into his pants. He took my hand and gently held it to his side, letting me feel the warmth of his ribs through the thin layer of cotton.

"I'm sorry," I whispered.

"Sorry for what?" he asked sweetly.

"Sorry I can't answer your questions," I said, still whispering vulnerably. "I don't even know what you're saying. I can't seem to think straight right now."

Collin hesitated for a few charged seconds before stooping down to literally toss me over his shoulder.

Epilogue
The following morning

I gained consciousness without moving or shifting at all. One minute I was dreaming, and the next, I was conscious. I opened my eyes just a crack the instant I woke up, and it dawned on me that I was in a real castle. I smiled sleepily at the thought. The room was comfortable but cool, and I found myself wrapped warmly in the elegant linens and warm comforter.

Without stirring, I focused on a ray of sunlight that was piercing through the curtains on the far side of the room. I smiled when I realized Collin was sitting over there with the sun shining down on him. He normally wore contacts, but he had on a pair of glasses as he stared at the screen of his laptop. His hair was falling over his eyebrow, and I felt the urge to reach out and run my fingers through it. I wanted him close to me so I could touch him.

I let out a little moan, letting him know I was awake, and I watched with delight as his head whipped up to see if I had indeed made a sound. He was sitting directly in the only sunlight in the room, so it was easy for me to see him, but hard for him to see me. He squinted in my direction like he was waiting to hear it again. I made another little noise, smiling because it was louder than the first one and I knew it would draw him to me.

Collin sprang off of his chair like it was on fire. He crossed the room, going over and not around obstacles like a couch and an ottoman to get to me. It was a beautiful and funny display of athleticism, and I giggled the whole time he ran to me, cracking up even harder when he came barreling into the bed. In one fluid motion, slid underneath the covers and snuggled up next to me.

"You're freezing," I said, giggling as he latched onto me.

"I didn't realize it would get this cool in here," he said. "I got up to take care of a few emails. I thought about lighting a fire, but you were sleeping so beautifully."

I stretched and positioned my face on his chest. "I don't mind if you wake me up," I said sleepily.

We stayed there for a few minutes of quiet comfort where we just held each other. I could feel his body temperature go from cold to warm, matching mine.

"Thank you for last night," I said, feeling blood rush to my face at the vulnerable feeling it gave me to say it. I was thankful that we weren't looking at each other.

Collin was silent for half a minute, but I stayed quiet because I knew he was thinking of what to say, or how to say it, or both. "Sarah, I, uh, last night... What I want to say is *thank you*."

I felt his hand come up to my head, holding me to his chest.

"I'm serious, Sarah, thank you. It makes me feel amazing that I'm the only one who gets to know you."

"You're welcome," I whispered. "Thank you for being so gentle."

I cuddled up next to him, and he settled into place with me. Just when we got comfortable, I lifted my head off of his chest so that I could stare at him. His eyes were mostly closed, but he squinted at me and smiled.

"I'm in love," I said.

"Tha's good, cause we're married," he said in perfect Dublinese.

I grinned at him and he returned it even though he was pretending to be sleepy.

"We're married," I agreed, testing out the words on my lips. I couldn't help but smile when I said it. "My husband, Collin," I said. "My husband, Collin," I repeated, using different fluctuation. "This is Collin Ross, my husband," I added in a fancy, somewhat British-sounding accent.

That one caused him to laugh out loud, and I took great pleasure in the sight. I thought about kissing him, and that brought another thought to mind.

"This is random," I said. "But Lu kissed someone at the wedding."

"Really?" he asked. "Who?"

"I don't know," I said. "She wouldn't own up to it, which was weird since she usually tells me stuff like that."

"Maybe nothing happened," Collin said.

"It did. I ran into her in the hallway, and I could tell she had just been kissing someone. It was obvious."

Collin shrugged. "Maybe it was Grant," he said, referring to one of our new friends from Ireland. "Or your brother."

"Yeah, I didn't think about Grant. It could have been him. I don't think it was Drake or Joe. She would have told me if that were the case, don't you think? I wonder why she didn't want to talk about it."

"Maybe she just didn't want to go into it on your wedding day."

"Yeah."

"Or maybe nothing happened."

"Oh, she'd been kissed," I said.

I smiled and stretched up to place my lips right on his. "I know because I'm an expert." I whispered.

"You are?"

"Uh-huh."

"Show me," he whispered.

So I did.

The End
(till book 2)

Thanks and love to my team ~ Chris, Jan, and Glenda

Made in the USA
Middletown, DE
14 August 2017